"If you wanted my attention, you certainly picked the dress for it," Nick said.

Jess turned to face him, knowing the truth of his words.

He stared at her dress with frank admiration. "How does it hide your . . . ah . . ."

"Prayer," she said, smiling at his consternation. His gaze seemed to heat her skin.

"Let's walk in the garden," he suggested, taking her hand and leading her outside. "You designed it, didn't you?" he asked.

"Yes. But I hope you didn't bring me out here to talk about business," Jess said.

He moved close to her, until their bodies were inches apart. "I brought you out here for this." With gentle force he lowered his mouth to hers, slipped his arms around her and drew her against him. He felt her hands on his shoulders, as if to push him away. Then, after a moment of hesitation, her nails sank into his shirt, and she parted her lips and offered him the sweetness of her mouth. In the longing of her kiss there was a need he'd never imagined, a passion hotter than a fire's heart. . . .

WHAT ARE *LOVESWEPT* ROMANCES?

They are stories of true romance and touching emotion. We believe those two very important ingredients are constants in our highly sensual and very believable stories in the *LOVESWEPT* line. Our goal is to give you, the reader, stories of consistently high quality that may sometimes make you laugh, sometimes make you cry, but are always fresh and creative and contain many delightful surprises within their pages.

Most romance fans read an enormous number of books. Those they truly love, they keep. Others may be traded with friends and soon forgotten. We hope that each *LOVESWEPT* romance will be a treasure—a "keeper." We will always try to publish

LOVE STORIES YOU'LL NEVER FORGET
BY AUTHORS YOU'LL ALWAYS REMEMBER

The Editors

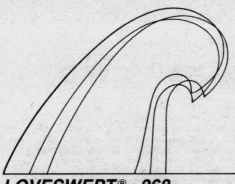

LOVESWEPT® • 268

Linda Cajio
Strictly Business

BANTAM BOOKS
TORONTO • NEW YORK • LONDON • SYDNEY • AUCKLAND

STRICTLY BUSINESS
A Bantam Book / July 1988

If you would be interested in receiving protective vinyl
covers for your Loveswept books, please write to this address
for information:

Loveswept
Bantam Books
P.O. Box 985
Hicksville, NY 11802

ISBN 0-553-21911-1

Published simultaneously in the United States and Canada

PRINTED IN THE UNITED STATES OF AMERICA

O   0 9 8 7 6 5 4 3 2 1

For Pat

One

What a shame he was gay.

Even the driving music, the high-pitched hysterical laughter, the roving spotlights couldn't distract Jess Brannen. Her gaze was riveted to the tall man standing near the doors of the banquet room. He was glaring at the young male dancer, aptly named Adonis, who was slowly peeling off his shirt to the screams of enthusiastic women. The lines of the man's mouth became even grimmer when the stripper, hips gyrating rhythmically, tossed the shirt onto one of the tables. Five women pounced on it, literally ripping it to shreds as each grappled for a souvenir.

From her place near the back of the room, Jess carefully watched for a reaction. His arms were folded across his chest, and she could see his body stiffen, the muscles of his jaw tighten.

His stony expression triggered a memory, and she realized she'd seen this man before. Immediately, she shifted so she no longer had a clear view of him. She prayed the same was true for him.

Although she'd never met Nick Mikaris, fastest-rising builder in the Philadelphia area, she had seen his picture in the business section of the newspaper several weeks ago. She had a meeting with Mikaris Tuesday morning to discuss her firm's doing the landscaping for his latest project, MeadowHill, and she didn't want him to recognize her as a spectator at a male strip show. Businesspeople could be very quirky about something like that.

But if it was Mikaris, why was *he* here?

Maybe she was worried for nothing, she thought. Maybe it wasn't he, just someone who looked like the picture. Photos could be deceiving. She decided to risk a peek.

It was he.

It was the same set of the jaw, but the picture didn't begin to do him justice. Although his features were too sharp for him to be truly handsome, he gave off an air of potent virility. She judged him to be about six feet in height. He was lean, with dark hair brushed back from his forehead. His simple pullover and gray slacks revealed the well-toned muscles of his body. He was a very attractive man—and definitely possessive of the dancer.

Suddenly Mikaris turned his head, and she found herself staring directly into his eyes. Even from twenty feet away, she could easily feel his gaze rake her. Her blood flowed hot and thick in blinding response, and her breasts ached almost painfully. Molten sensations swirled around her belly and thighs.

With a mighty effort, Jess ducked her head. She immediately took a huge gulp of her drink, but the chilled Bahama Mama didn't help. Her face was flushed with embarrassment, and she groaned to herself. Of all the idiotic things to do! She hoped he hadn't had a good enough look at her to actually identify her. To insure he wouldn't, she planned to look entirely different for the meeting—exactly like a businesswoman who would be shocked at the very idea of attending a show like this one. If only she hadn't been so intrigued by him in the first place . . . .

She must be drunk, she decided, frowning at her glass. It was only her second drink, and the fruity concoction was supposed to be fairly innocent. But the combination of the drinks, little dinner, and total exhaustion was making her silly. Her movements did seem awkward, and her head was too heavy for her neck. That was it, she thought in relief. She was just a little bit tipsy. Maybe more than a little, she conceded. But that explained her unusual reaction to the man.

"Jess! He's at our table!" Although her best friend, Sandy Fitzgerald, was literally rubbing shoulders with her, Sandy had to shout over the din.

In a panic, Jess looked around, then shivered with relief when she saw Sandy meant the dancer, Adonis. He was performing directly in front of reserved, elegant Gwen. Laughter overtook Jess when Gwen pulled the linen tablecloth over her head. Gwen was taking Sandy's practical joke well, Jess thought.

The five women, Sandy, Gwen, Adele, Miranda, and herself, had been close friends since they'd attended Bryn Mawr College together, and every year one of the group played a practical joke on another. This time Gwen had been Sandy's victim. Dinner and gambling in Atlantic City had actually been a "Ladies' Night" show at the Breakers Casino/Hotel— the very last thing Philadelphia socialite Gwen

Halloran would ever attend. This joke had been perfect and diabolical in its simplicity, Jess thought, and Gwen had been truly caught. Although they had all been shocked initially by the male strippers, they had soon relaxed and begun enjoying themselves, even laughing at the men's outrageousness. It was innocent fun, Jess decided, wiping the tears from her eyes.

Adonis moved closer to her, and her mirth immediately subsided. But the dancer settled on Sandy for his next private audience, and she started to relax . . . .

Her entire body froze when the good-looking dancer turned to her. He gave her a lazy smile, while his hips began to circle slowly. She hadn't realized how tiny his G-string was. The damn thing was almost nonexistent!

"Oh, no!" she moaned, and buried her face in her hands.

"Stop being a prude, Jess!" Sandy shouted in her ear.

"I'm not!" Jess lied, laughing with good-natured humiliation.

She turned to her friend and spread her fingers wide so she could see perfectly. Sandy burst into laughter. Jess didn't turn back to the dancer, however. One look had been more than enough.

But Adonis moved closer until he was actually bumping her chair. She instantly closed her fingers together and wished the floor would open up and swallow her. She had to get rid of him.

Snatching up her purse, she grabbed the first bill her fingers touched and shoved it at the dancer. It was a twenty.

Sandy leaned forward and asked dryly, "Would you like change?"

"A Brannen doesn't wait for change, darling," Jess drawled in her best Bryn Mawr voice. She didn't have a smaller bill, and even if she had, she'd be damned before she'd hunt for it.

Adonis kissed her on the cheek and danced away.

"We're blowing our conservative image to Hades!" Gwen shouted, finally emerging from the tablecloth. Her carefully styled hair wasn't even mussed.

"You are," Jess screamed over the pounding music. "I have to keep up the family image of eccentricity!"

"What?"

Jess waved her hand. Her throat was already raw, and it would never carry past three people. She watched Gwen nod in understanding about the noise level. Anyway, Gwen already knew what Philadelphia's first families thought of Jessica Brannen. All the Brannens were noted for flaunting convention upon occasion. Still, her career as a landscaper raised more eyebrows than usual. Why it should, she didn't know. Doing what she liked and had a talent for made a lot more sense than working at some job she hated.

She chuckled to herself. People might frown, but it didn't stop them from asking her to landscape their properties.

Suddenly, she felt as if someone were staring at her, and glanced toward the doors. Mikaris whirled on his heel and left the room.

Jess sighed. She hoped she wouldn't pay for this night out.

And in more ways than one.

•   •   •

Nick Mikaris strode through the hotel lobby and into the bar. He needed fortification for the upcoming battle with Tony.

"Whiskey. Straight up," he told the bartender.

When his drink arrived, he just stared at it. Booze wouldn't help what he was feeling. Damn Tony, he thought, curling his hands into tight fists. He could understand his brother's need for financial independence. But why did Tony have to take his clothes off in front of hundreds of screaming women to achieve it?

He thought of one woman in there, slim and dark and ethereal, who had stared at him so boldly and made him forget everything but her for a long moment. He cursed and brought his wandering attention back to the problem of Tony. It didn't matter if the job paid the tuition for law school, he thought angrily. Didn't Tony realize how this would follow him through his career?

Despite the closed padded doors on the other side of the lobby, he could hear the shrieking women. He deliberately relaxed his body and finally admitted the truth. It was all his fault. At twenty-eight, he hadn't been prepared to raise a sixteen-year-old boy. He had made mistakes over the past seven years. Too many, obviously. Somehow, somewhere, despite all his care, he had done something that had warped his brother.

And somehow, somewhere, he would have to find the exact right thing that would persuade Tony to give up stripping.

Months of yelling hadn't worked so far, and Nick thought of his hotel room with grim satisfaction. Tony was supposed to be staying at a motel with the show, but Nick vowed to keep his hardheaded brother captive here all night until he pounded some sense into him.

"I don't think it's fair that Jess can get out of it, but I can't," Gwen protested after the show was over.

"That's because you're the 'jokee,' " Sandy said, rising from her chair. "You, my dear, have to go backstage and meet the guys in the—"

"Buff?" Jess offered with a straight face.

"Thank you." Sandy tilted her head in acknowledgment, then turned back to Gwen. "Jess was up at five so she could finish the Howards' place before coming to the shore. I think we can let her off this one time." Sandy patted Jess's shoulder. "We'll go pick up the room keys, then come back and get you, okay?"

"In the meantime, I'll take a nap," Jess said, smiling. "Try not to be an animal, Gwen."

"Thanks a lot," Gwen grumbled, and was swept away to her fate.

Jess giggled. Getting out of meeting the male strippers had almost been too easy. Good thing it had, she thought, leaning her elbow on the table. She didn't have the energy to get out of her chair, let alone the desire to meet nearly naked men. Besides, nothing would ever rival the expression on Gwen's face when she'd seen the first dancer in action.

Closing her eyes, Jess listened with pleasure as the room quickly cleared out and near silence descended. Every muscle in her body ached as if she had run the Boston Marathon. A dense fog had enshrouded her brain. If breathing wasn't involuntary, she'd be in big trouble. She was paying now for her twenty-one-hour day. Leave it to Serena Howard to demand an entire acre of back lawn be dug up and resodded in one day, she thought. Thank goodness Sandy had arranged for the group to stay at the hotel tonight. She never would have survived the long drive back to her home in Yardley, Pennsylvania. All she had to do was stay upright until they came back for her.

Jess smiled at the thought of a bed. She couldn't wait to peel off her clothes and climb between the sheets. She'd tuck the covers against her chin . . . burrow her face in the soft pillows . . .

She became aware of laughter, all-out female laughter. A corner of her mind, disturbed by it, wished they would stop so she could sleep.

"Jess! *Jess!*"

She forced one eye open. All she could see was a white cloth stretching forever. "Wha . . . ?"

"Wake up." Somebody was shaking her shoulder. "Jess, wake up so you can go to bed."

The last word penetrated her groggy brain, and she forced the other eye open. She was staring at a linen-covered table. She gratefully closed her eyes, puzzling over why she had dreamed she was the guest of honor at a Chinese funeral. Suddenly, naked men danced across her numb mind. She smiled. This dream was going to be a doozy.

"Jess!"

She bolted upright and stared uncomprehendingly at the crowd that appeared magically on the other side of the table.

"What?"

Sandy's face swam to the forefront. Jess frowned as she unsuccessfully tried to bring her friend into focus.

"Jess, honey." Sandy's voice came from a great distance. "Think you can make it upstairs?" She was laughing, and Jess wondered why.

"No problem, Sandy," she mumbled, and laid her head back down on the table.

"Let's get her up."

Hands helped her out of her chair. The entire room tilted violently and she groaned.

"Maybe we ought to get some coffee into her."

"Anything but that!" she gasped, turning her head to glare at the person who would make such an appalling suggestion.

The room tilted again, and she immediately closed her eyes. She finally reopened them when her stomach settled, this time keeping her gaze straight ahead. The room only rocked gently that way.

"Ready?"

She nodded, and realized her mistake when a reminder to keep her head as still as possible crashed through her. She obeyed.

"Ready," she muttered.

Despite the hands grasping her upper arms, she staggered around the table. Laughter boomed through her ears. She forced herself to continue putting one foot in front of the other, hoping to get away from the painful noise. But with each step, she was positive she'd fall flat on her face any second.

"She's not going to make it!"

Jess took the remark for a command, and gratefully let her knees buckle under her.

"Grab her!"

She was unceremoniously hauled upright.

"Look at her! I think she had too much. This will never work, Sandy."

"Yes, it will. I've planned it perfectly."

"Sssh! You'll give it away!"

"No, I won't. Jess. Jess!"

Jess tried to focus on the voice calling her name.

"Do you know what I'm talking about?"

Jess hadn't even attempted to follow the conversation. All she could think about was lying horizontally. Lord, but she was tired.

"Jess, the elevators are just a little bit farther." It was Sandy's voice again. "You can do it!"

"Wanna bet?" Jess muttered, concentrating on the seamed double doors in front of her. Odd that her house had suddenly acquired an elevator, she thought dimly, then wished the people behind her would shut up. Every sound was like a knife plunging into her. Her stomach lurched sideways now with each step, and her head weighed at least two tons. A voice in her brain, though, was chanting wildly, "One more step to the bed." She hung on desperately to the thought.

The elevator ride was merciless. Fortunately, once off the thing, it was a short stagger down the hallway to a room. Someone opened the door, and Jess gazed in awe at the wide, inviting bed. The blessed promise was there before her in all its glory.

Unexpectedly, something inside her protested crossing the threshold. Jess ignored it, and lurched forward. She'd kill anyone or anything who stood between her and the bed. Flopping onto the soft enveloping mattress, she closed her eyes. At last, she thought hazily. Peace, comfort, and sleep.

She drifted off to the sounds of hysterical laughter.

"Dammit, Nick! How many times do I have to explain to you," Tony snapped, clenching his glass of cola. "The whole purpose of this job is that *I'm* the one who pays for school. I do it. Not you. Not anybody else."

Nick glared across the small table at his brother. "There are plenty of other jobs, much more respectable jobs, that pay well."

"Not like this!"

"You'll regret this one for the rest of your life. What if sometime in the future you want to be a judge? You won't get appointed with . . . stripping in your background. And you don't have to do it. I've told you I'll pay the tuition for school. That's final, Tony. End of discussion."

Tony leaned back in his chair and eyed his brother sourly. "Stop being a prude, Nick, and look at this from a purely financial angle."

Nick swallowed his drink in one gulp. "I am. And I'm not a prude!"

Tony laughed. "Nick, you're so conservative that you used to call dates 'business meetings.' "

Nick gaped at Tony. He hadn't realized his brother had caught on to his ruse of years ago. Okay, so maybe he'd been a little extreme when he'd first divorced Janet. He clamped his jaw closed at the thought of his ex-wife. "You were only sixteen, Tony, and you didn't need any more disruption to cope with. Besides, there weren't that many dates."

"I was seventeen by then, and not stupid." Tony waved a hand in a dismissive gesture. "The point is that I pay for law school, Nick. And I'll only have to work three nights a week to do it. I'll have plenty of time for studying." He leaned forward and said earnestly, "I gave this a lot of thought, and I know exactly what I'm doing and what it means for my future. It's going to be all the sweeter because I was the one who worked for it."

"But—"

"No buts, Nick! Even if I were willing, you can't pay for the tuition. You've got everything tied up in those custom homes you're building. You're strapped enough right now, and I'll be damned before I strap you any further. It's my turn to pay. The job is fine, and I have enough sense to stay away from the ladies, if that's what you're worried about."

"Tony—"

"No. Face it, Nick. I'm twenty-three, and I'm all grown up. You have to stop being a parent." Tony stood. "Now, this is the end of the discussion. It's two in the morning, and I have to get back to the motel and get some sleep. Tomorrow afternoon, we're leaving for a show in Baltimore."

He walked away.

Rising, Nick cursed aloud and threw money down on the table. He quickly caught up with his brother.

"Tony . . ."

"Give it a break, Nick." His brother smiled to soften the words. "Come on, I'll walk you up to your room."

Nick sighed in defeat. He knew if he pressed the issue he'd drive Tony away from him. It was the last thing he wanted. Maybe Tony felt the same, since their arguments always ended before irreparable damage was done.

"Come over and have breakfast with me before

you go," he said as they crossed the lobby. "We can pick up where we left off."

Tony grinned. "Anybody ever tell you you're a wonderful, kindly brother?"

"Not lately."

"Good, I wouldn't want to spoil my record. By the way, thanks for letting me use your shower earlier. I'm drenched after a show."

"I bet," Nick grumbled, remembering his brief introduction to his brother's work.

Tony wagged a finger. "Watch out, Nicolas Mikaris. You're going to fall off that pedestal of yours very soon, and I'm going to be there to see it."

Nick stared at him. There was smug amusement in his brother's tone, and his eyes were alight with mischief.

"You look a little too pleased about that."

Tony attempted to smother his amusement under a shrug. He wasn't entirely successful. "At least you didn't punch me in the jaw tonight. For a moment there, I thought you were going to."

Nick cuffed him lightly. "Don't tempt me, pal. Adonis! Lord help us!"

Tony laughed. "Hey, it's my real name."

Nick couldn't deny that. The name on Tony's birth certificate was Athoni, which, unfortunately, meant Adonis in Greek. If Nick had his way, Tony would be named Hector or Wilbur or something. The less said about Adonis, the better.

When they reached his hotel room, Nick unlocked the door and flipped on the light. He noticed Tony staring slack-jawed into the room. He turned around to see what had caught his brother's attention. Except for one side of the bedspread being slightly rumpled, the room was as it had been when he'd left it earlier.

"Did you sit on the bed when you came up for the shower?" he asked.

"Oh! Ah . . . yes." Tony straightened. "I . . . ah . . . called Bill to tell him I'd be late. Hope you don't mind."

"No problem."

His brother blinked, and to Nick's surprise, peered around the room again. "Right. Well, I'll see you in the morning."

"Around ten?"

Tony gave the room a last searching glance, then nodded.

"Are you all right?" Nick asked, puzzled by Tony's odd behavior.

"Fine. Fine. I'll see you tomorrow."

Nick closed the door behind him and shrugged. Maybe he'd been too tired tonight to argue effectively with Tony. There had been several problems at the job site today, and as the owner of Mikaris Builders, he had been the only one able to fix them. For a while, he'd almost thought he wouldn't be able to get away to see Tony. Not that it had done any good, he thought with irritation. Things were still at their usual stalemate.

Yanking off his pullover, he flexed an aching shoulder and decided what he needed was a good night's sleep. He pulled down the covers on the bed, shed the rest of his clothes, and climbed between the cool sheets.

The image of the woman he'd spotted in the banquet room flashed through his mind. She had been captivating, with her shining brown hair and large innocent eyes. Her features had been almost angelic in their delicacy, and yet he'd sensed a waiting fire in her. It had teased him, tantalized his sanity.

She was probably married.

He blocked out her image and closed his eyes.

Lying across the bathroom floor, Jess hugged the cool porcelain of the toilet bowl to her flushed cheek in relief and gratitude. It was so smooth and cool. Her stomach was finally calming down. It ought to, she thought absently. Nothing was in it now.

She lay there for the longest time, almost dozing, until she finally realized that comforting as the bowl was, it wasn't comfortable. Pulling the last of her energy together, she sat up. She became aware that she was still in her clothes and her purse was hanging on her arm. She dropped her purse on the floor and stripped off her dress. Amazing, she thought. She couldn't care less that she'd fallen asleep in a Rudolpho, but the dress didn't show a wrinkle. Finally, she staggered back into the bedroom, tossed the dress and purse over a chair, and slowly settled into the bed. As she closed her eyes, she vowed to never, never, never do one of these practical jokes again.

The aftermath was a killer.

Two

Jess slowly surfaced from a dead sleep. Natural light, not too bright, filtered behind her closed eyelids, telling her the sun had been up for quite some time. She smiled, remembering her dream about a very sexy man. It had been so vivid that she could still feel his body curved spoonlike around hers. Of course, it was a perfect fit . . .

A certain part of her dream was pressed a little too realistically to her hips. She opened her eyes. Her first thought was that someone had completely redecorated her room during the night. Then she became all too aware that she wasn't in her own bed.

And she wasn't alone.

"This ain't Kansas, Toto," she whispered under her breath as she inched away from the sleeping man. Her heart pounded with fear, her stomach churned with panic, and her head felt like a marching band was going full blast inside it.

What, she wondered frantically, had she done last

night? And where were Sandy and the others? All she remembered was going to the show, being sick, and collapsing in a bed. *Alone.*

So where had the man come from?

She decided not to wait around for a trip down memory lane. She just wanted to get out of there as quietly as possible, go home, and yell at herself for the rest of her life. Slowly, she slipped a leg over the bed—

"What the hell!" a deep voice exclaimed behind her.

Jess leaped off the bed and whipped around. She stared in astonishment.

"You!" she said at the same time as Nick Mikaris.

Jess blinked. She knew why she was saying it, but why was *he* saying it?

Glaring, Mikaris got out of the bed, pulling the bedspread around his hips as he did. She blushed hotly at the flash of a bare hip before the quilted material hid his essentials. His shoulders were broader than she'd first thought, and his chest was covered with dark curling hair that arrowed down his stomach before disappearing beyond.

Forcing her gaze away, she wished the building would collapse around her. If she'd thought last night might prove embarrassing, this was infinitely worse. She tried to think logically around a blinding headache, hoping to come up with a sensible explanation for why he was in her room.

She wracked her brain, but she had no recollection of meeting or talking with him. She couldn't remember anything past collapsing into an empty bed. Of all the men in the world for this to happen with, why Nick Mikaris? How would he ever accept a business relationship with her after being in her bed?

A thought occurred to her, and she glanced down at her slip and panty hose. She was still dressed! Two drinks shouldn't turn a normal person into a lusting animal. And the man was gay, for goodness' sake! She'd seen that preference with her own eyes. Maybe there was hope for her yet. Still, when she'd first awakened she was aware of a definite male response to their closeness.

She felt his gaze burn through her slip, and realized its flimsy satin material wasn't exactly a formidable barrier. Flushing, she tugged at the blanket on the bed to cover herself more thoroughly. It wouldn't pull out from where it was tucked under the mattress. She snatched up a pillow instead and pressed it against her middle. It was better than nothing.

"Who are you and how did you get into this room?" he demanded.

"The hotel put me in this room," she said, puzzled by his second question.

"Then they've got terrific room service. But I didn't order room service, sweetheart, so how did you get into my room?"

She gaped at him. "Your . . . But this is my room!"

"Your room?" He frowned at her, then snatched something off the dresser and held it up. It was a key. "It says ten twenty-six. That was the room I was given when I registered. Where's your key?"

"I—I don't know." She glanced around the room. It certainly looked like the same one she'd been put in last night. "I'm here with friends, and they registered for me . . . Wait a minute."

She walked over to the chair and pulled her purse out from underneath her dress. She rummaged through it, hoping to find a hotel key, but none was there.

"My friends must have the key," she muttered, a flush rising in her cheeks again.

"I think I just made some new friends," he drawled, eyeing her lustfully.

There had to be a logical explanation here, she thought. "Maybe there was a mix-up at the desk and that's how we wound up in the same room."

"Sounds like my kind of mix-up."

He looked as if he were about to take full advantage of the mix-up. She inhaled deeply to fight back her rising panic, telling herself she wouldn't *not* remember if something had happened between them. Much as she wished she didn't, she had to tell him who she was and remind him of their meeting on Tuesday.

"It's definitely a mix-up," she said, attempting a casual smile. It didn't feel casual. "But I hope you have a sense of humor. You see—"

She was interrupted by a knock at the door.

"I bet it's the manager, coming to tell *us* there's a mix-up," he said, striding over to the door. "Like we haven't figured that out for ourselves."

He unlocked the door and opened it. The stripper, Adonis, was standing on the threshold.

"Tony!"

Jess pressed a shaking hand against her eyes. The lover! Slowly, she sank down onto the edge of the mattress. *This is another fine mess you've gotten yourself into,* she thought.

"Well, well, well," Tony said. Jess lowered her hand

just in time to see him stroll into the room. "Who have we here, Nick?"

"I haven't found out yet," Nick said, shutting the door with a bang.

"You mean you never even asked?" Tony exclaimed in a shocked voice. "A gentleman always asks, Nick."

"Dammit, Tony, don't tease. You ought to know better, after the talk we had last night—"

Jess broke in. "Ah . . . excuse me."

The men turned toward her.

"This is not what you're thinking," she began. The younger man must be devastated by what seemed like a betrayal, she thought. She'd been in his position herself, and knew only too well how hurt and humiliated he must feel. She prayed that Mikaris would just be momentarily embarrassed that she knew about his sexual preference. Unfortunately, she didn't think calling on the Almighty would help. She had a feeling her chances for the job were one big zip. "There seems to have been some kind of mix-up by the hotel, and your . . . ah, anyway, somehow we were given the same room."

"Given the same room?" Tony asked, arching his eyebrows in clear disbelief.

"We only slept together—" Jess exclaimed, then realized how that sounded.

"Shared a bed," Nick corrected.

"We didn't know it . . . we were sleeping . . ." She snapped her jaw shut in frustration, counted to five, and said, "Look, it's just a foul-up on the hotel's part. But I know how it looks to you to catch a . . . loved one in a hotel room with another woman. I mean man. No, woman." She groaned, finding it difficult to keep the genders straight. "We didn't do anything! After all, Mr. . . . well, he's gay, and you're gay. It's just a very innocent mix-up, that's all—"

A bellow of pure outrage blasted through the room. Shocked, Jess stared wide-eyed at Nick.

"I'm not gay!" he shouted. "Why the hell would anyone think I'm gay?"

"But you looked gay last night!" she said, hopelessly confused. "At the show . . . staring at him like—"

"This," he said through clenched teeth, "is my brother! My *brother*! And I wasn't staring at him the way I was staring at *you*!"

There was a moment of charged silence, then Tony burst into laughter. It took Jess a moment to realize that he was laughing. In fact, he was leaning against the wall as if he couldn't hold himself upright.

"You were perfect," he said, gasping. "You thought Nick was gay! I couldn't have done better if I'd written a script."

It suddenly dawned on her that this had to be a joke. A practical joke!

"I'm the jokee?" she asked in shock. "Dammit! I'm really this year's victim, right?"

Still laughing, Tony nodded.

Jess started to laugh from sheer nerves. She couldn't help it, even though she had to press her palm against the top of her head to stop the pain her laughter caused. Sandy had suckered her beautifully, she thought, and she would kill her good friend later.

"I should have known it," she finally said, shaking her head.

"What the hell is this about a joke?" Nick asked angrily.

"Your downfall, Nick," Tony said. "And it was even better than I'd planned."

"My downfall?" He glared at Tony. "Do you mean you planned this little stunt?"

Tony grinned. "Let's just say I took a joke one step farther." He turned to Jess. "I borrowed Sandy's joke to play one on my brother, Ms. Brannen."

At her name, Nick instantly shifted his gaze to her. Jess realized that he hadn't been amused at being the victim of a practical joke, and he wasn't about to start now. The joke wasn't funny anymore. Not funny at all.

Fate, she decided, had a warped sense of humor. Facing Nick, she pulled her courage together and lifted her chin. "I started to tell you before that I'm Jess Brannen, but we were interrupted. It would seem, Mr. Mikaris, that our interview was moved up to this morning. Now if you'll excuse me, I'd like to get dressed, go home, and have a good scream."

"But I don't understand," Sandy exclaimed into the phone. "The joke was supposed to be that you'd wake up to find a man in your room who would act like you'd picked him up. You've never done that in your life. But it was supposed to be Tony Mikaris! I didn't even know Nick was going to be there."

"Well, he was." Jess wished she could yank her friend through the telephone wire and into her kitchen. It would be lovely to put her hands around Sandy's throat. "This is just great. I had a meeting with Mikaris to get the landscaping job for the model of these custom farmettes he's building near Washington's Crossing. It's called MeadowHill."

"I didn't know that. I mean I know about Meadow-Hill. Marty's one of Nick's backers. But I didn't know you were up for the landscaping job."

"Your wonderful husband Marty recommended me!" Jess resisted the urge to scream in frustration. Anyway, she'd done that on the two-hour drive home, and it hadn't helped.

"But you didn't tell me, and neither did Marty," Sandy wailed.

"I didn't tell you because I have this stupid superstition that I'll jinx a job if I blab." Jess rubbed her forehead. "I was going to tell you after I got it. I don't know why Marty didn't tell you."

"He probably thought you would want to be the one to tell me. He's like that, the idiot. Jess, I'm sorry the joke backfired. Really sorry. Look, it's not that bad. Just explain to Nick—"

"Sandy," Jess interrupted, "I thought the man was gay! If he didn't have a sense of humor on that one, he's certainly not going to be Mr. Understanding about the rest of it."

"You thought . . ." Sandy burst into laughter. "Lord, Jess! You must have hit him in his male pride. Nick's got a lot of that."

Jess groaned. "I doubt that it was the high point in his life. But, dammit, Sandy! This is all your fault!"

"I wasn't the one who thought he was gay, Jess."

"I don't mean that part!" Jess wished she could forget that she'd ever thought it of Nick. "Everything would have been fine if you'd found a more reliable participant than Tony. He's the one who made the switch."

There was a long pause before Sandy asked, "Are you planning on speaking to me ever again?"

"I don't know."

"I forgave you when that damn mariachi band played for four hours on my anniversary, Jess," Sandy wheedled. "At one in the morning. Believe me, that wasn't easy, especially when they interrupted our reenactment of the wedding night."

Jess giggled.

"Four hours, Jess. No amount of money would buy them off, either. I thought Marty would go crazy. But I forgave you. Really and truly, in my heart of hearts, I forgave you for that one."

"Since you put it like that . . ."

When Jess finally hung up the phone, she stared at it in disgust. What a disaster. It was obvious that Sandy had planned an entirely different ending to the joke, but it hadn't worked out that way.

She pulled out a stool at the kitchen counter and sat down. Dammit! She had really wanted that job on the Mikaris model. It would have established her as a legitimate landscaper. Nick Mikaris wasn't someone who would hire her only so he could say afterward, "Would you believe it? Jess Brannen laid my sod."

None of her friends or family took her landscaping business seriously. To an extent, she couldn't blame them. After all, she'd grown up with three trust funds. Arranging flowers was an acceptable hobby for someone with her background, but spreading fertilizer wasn't. She'd already done the acceptable thing—prep school, college, marriage, charity work. It had taken a humiliating divorce before she'd realized that the acceptable wasn't all it was cracked up to be. Jess smiled wryly. Her mother had warned her.

Shortly after the divorce, she had needed something normal. Something that wouldn't raise eyebrows or be splattered in the gossip columns of the newspapers. By accident, she had discovered landscaping. Nothing was more satisfying for her than to take the bare earth and create pleasure for the senses from it. All she asked for was a little respect while she was doing it. When Sandy's husband, Marty, one of Mikaris's investors, had suggested she see Nick, she'd jumped at the chance. After a couple of years in operation, her business was ready to move up, and she'd been looking for the perfect job to put her over the edge. Mikaris was only building ten homes, five-acre farmettes actually, but the job had sounded perfect. And best of all, it would have been two professionals working together. He would customize the homes to the owners' specifications, and she would customize the properties. She had known her background might hamper her, and she had asked Marty not to say anything, planning to tell Mikaris herself. After she got the job.

Now, because of a dumb practical joke that had backfired, she'd lost the opportunity altogether.

"Damn! The whole thing blown in one morning because of a silly joke," she muttered to herself.

She remembered how she had grabbed her dress and purse and run out of the room, leaving her shoes behind. *Real professional, Jess*, she thought in frustration. She'd stuck him with the hotel bill, too.

He'd never subcontract the landscaping to her now. How would she ever explain the mess in one breath and persuade him she was a businesswoman in the next? And what about her unexpected yet strong attraction to Mikaris? She considered that and decided that being attracted to him might have complicated things a little, but she could have handled it. He was hard-edged, not at all the kind of man she usually gravitated toward, or ever thought she would be attracted to. And knowing what she knew about herself, she had no alternative but to ignore her attraction . . .

Jess straightened, as a thought occurred to her. She was a mature woman, but she hadn't been thinking like one. Why shouldn't she keep the interview? She had simply been caught up in a practical joke between brothers. Granted, it was embarrassing, but it had nothing to do with the job. Granted, she found him attractive, but she had enough barriers erected to keep her in balance. It wouldn't be easy to face him again, but she'd be a fool not to try. The MeadowHill project would make her name in landscaping.

After all, what really mattered was that the man needed a landscaper. She was a landscaper, and a damn good one.

Now all she needed to do was persuade Nick Mikaris of that.

Three

Perched atop the unfinished roof of his model house, Nick watched a red BMW pull onto the construction site and stop next to the office trailer.

Jess Brannen emerged gracefully from the car and into the cool April day. She was dressed in a cream-colored suit and sensible low-heeled shoes. She pulled a large portfolio from the car, then looked around the site, taking in the house whose exterior was nearly finished. Land had been cleared for four more. Leisurely surveying her, he had to admit that she possessed the best legs he'd ever seen. From under the hem of her skirt, smooth calves tapered into trim ankles . . .

Suddenly, he became aware of whistles and cat-calls from his workers.

"Back to work, guys," he ordered, not liking the way they were eyeing her. The male appreciation was instantly replaced by the racket of busy hammers and saws.

As he climbed down a ladder, Nick admitted that he hadn't expected her to keep the appointment, not after the other morning. He really ought to throw her off the site. Over the weekend he'd discovered a few disturbing things about Jess Brannen. She liked to involve herself in silly practical jokes. The one in Atlantic City was hardly the first. Her family was "old" Philadelphia money, something his lawyer, Marty Fitzgerald, had neglected to tell him earlier. And she'd only worked with single homes before, probably friends of her parents.

Still, he hadn't been able to rid himself of the vision of her as she'd been that morning. Dark, dark hair had tumbled about her shoulders, and translucent silk had barely hidden her delicious curves. She could easily drive a man to insanity . . . and satisfaction.

She had thought he was gay.

That irritated him beyond reason. He knew he shouldn't hold the incident in Atlantic City against her. The simple fact was that he needed a professional, experienced landscaper for his homes and Jess Brannen didn't qualify for the job.

"Good morning, Mr. Mikaris," she said as he approached her.

He took his time removing his hard hat and tucking it under his arm. "You forgot your shoes the other morning, Ms. Brannen."

"I'm not here for my shoes," she said, unruffled. "We had an appointment at ten o'clock to discuss my firm's doing the landscaping for these homes. It's ten o'clock."

"Three days ago you woke up in my bed," he said bluntly.

"The victim of a practical joke. Both of us were. But why that should make a difference—"

"It doesn't."

He stared at her, helplessly admiring the sun streaks highlighting her hair. Threads of pastel pink and blue ran through the material of her suit, and the high collar of her silk blouse was wrapped around her slender neck. Delicate perfume tantalized his senses, and he suddenly became aware of the strong odor of the tar splattering his old jeans and denim jacket. He decided he'd be damned before this woman put him at a disadvantage.

"My brother," he continued, his voice cold, "whose occupation I dislike, explained to me that he thought it would be funny to put you in my room."

"Aha," she murmured.

"But practical jokes are your specialty, aren't they, Ms. Brannen?"

"I thought that wasn't supposed to make a difference," she said, arching an eyebrow.

He'd fallen into that one, he thought, irritated. "Marty neglected to tell me you've never done a job this big before. I need someone who knows what she's doing with this property. An experienced professional. I don't have the time or money to waste on an amateur."

"I see." He watched her glance around again and admitted that he admired her for showing up after Atlantic City. Waking up with a stranger could be embarrassing as hell for some women. He remembered the way she had scurried out of the hotel room. She *had* been embarrassed, but that hadn't stopped her.

"It will be a lovely Elizabethan farmhouse when

it's finished," she said, surprising him with a dazzling smile. "Unique, actually. An old-fashioned rose garden fronting the structure would be stunning. And authentic. Roses were extremely popular ornamentals during the reign of Elizabeth the First. Here, let me show you what I mean."

She unzipped her portfolio and laid it flat on the hood of her car. A series of photographs carelessly spilled out. Nick stared at pictures of beautiful estates with formal front gardens, intricate topiary, and elegant patios done in a riot of living color.

"Your work?" he asked.

"Yes," she said as she flipped through the sketches in a side pocket. "I did a row of homes in Radnor last year. The one with the topiary is the Barkeley estate."

"The bankers?"

"One of them. Vivian Barkeley, actually. Nice lady. She's a widow."

Jess was good, he admitted reluctantly, and her clientele impeccable.

"Ah, here it is." She pulled out a drawing. "I drove by here over the weekend and did up a rough sketch of the rose garden."

She handed it to him. It was a nearly perfect reproduction of the house with a rose garden fronting it. Beautiful old names of the various strains leaped out at him: damask, Persian, rugosa, sweetbriar. She had even done an overview of the garden so one could see the sunburst symmetry of the beds and walkways fanning out from a centerpiece sundial.

"A formal rose garden would add to the old-world charm of the house," she went on. "Please pardon me for saying this, but it would be too bad if this property wound up looking like any other development model."

Nick frowned. "What do you mean, Ms. Brannen?"

She smiled. "Call me Jess. Well, this is where the landscaping should really shine. You need a landscaper who understands not only the setting, but the type of people buying the homes. What their wants are, the kind of care they're willing to pay for or to give the property themselves in order to make their homes showplaces. Unfortunately, there's a no-frills trend among my colleagues these days. No matter what the house, they all seem to get five junipers, three evergreens, and a couple of azaleas for color. Without fail, the saplings are two silver maples, one oak, and a willow, if you're lucky. There's nothing wrong with that, mind you." She chuckled dryly. "In fact, it's easy and cheap. But I think it's a sin not to take the little extra care and expense to do a place right."

"It'll be done right," he snapped, although he was disturbed. He'd spoken with another landscaper, and the man had mentioned junipers, silver maples, and azaleas.

"That's good." She looked around again and sighed. "I really would have loved this project. I can already see flagstone walkways among the roses, and maybe one or two stone benches, all radiating from a sundial in the center of the garden. The house really needs the ornamentals and perennials that very few bother with these days—real, true landscaping that expresses the timelessness of nature . . . ."

Her voice trailed away, and all Nick could imagine was cool beauty in the winter and delicate color in the summer. He had wanted to build beyond the ordinary box house, and she was describing land-scaping to match.

"That proves you've got an eye for the job," he said, hoping to dispel the disturbing notion. "I've got everything sunk into this project, plus investors to please. I can't afford someone who might leave me with a half-finished property because she doesn't have the experience to handle the job. I need a reli-able landscaper. I'm sorry, Jess, but I don't think you're that person."

She straightened away from her car and lifted her chin. "I'll make you a bet. Hire me, and if I don't do the job in the time allotted or to your satisfaction, in any way, you don't pay me. Better still, not only do you not pay me, but I pay you a fine of five thousand dollars, *and* I'll pay for another landscaper to finish the job."

"Ten thousand," he said, wondering how far she would commit herself.

"Agreed. And it holds for your home buyers, too, if I don't deliver on time and to their satisfaction."

He shouldn't, Nick thought as he gazed into her wide brown eyes. She was trouble, and in more than one way. Still, she sounded sincere and committed. Marty had recommended her, and he had given good advice in the past. It was tempting, too, to see if she could pull off the bet. Everything about her was so damned tempting, from her calm exterior to the fire he knew was inside her.

"One mistake," he warned, "one time you're not professional, and I fire you."

"Write it in the contract and I'll sign it, Mr. Mikaris."

He hesitated for a moment, then made up his mind. "Done. And it's Nick."

She grinned and held out her hand. "You've got a deal, Nick."

He took her hand in his. It was warm and soft and totally feminine. A rush of primitive desire surged through him.

In that instant, he knew he'd just made the worst mistake of his life.

As Jess tramped around the farmhouse the next morning, she smiled with satisfaction. This was it, she thought. A real job. The perfect job to establish her business as legitimate. She turned to her two trusted employees. Both Duane and Roger were in their early twenties and looked like a pair of linebackers for the Philadelphia Eagles. Over the past two years, she'd come to think of them as oversized younger brothers.

"What do you think, guys?" she asked, grinning at them.

"I think you're a crazy lady," Duane said, staring at the piles of dirt pushed every which way on the property. "Six weeks isn't enough time to do the sprinkler system, the plantings, the sod—"

"It has to be," she said firmly. "The interior will be done by then, and that's when Mr. Mikaris plans to open it as a model. We've got to have the landscaping ready. Everything."

"We can do the front in that time," Roger said. "No problem there. But the back . . . I don't know, Jess."

"If I have to, I'll subcontract the final ground contouring and the sod work," she said. "But he'll want something just as elaborate for the back. I figure to use the fountain trick there."

The young men chuckled.

A voice interrupted them. "Good morning."

Jess spun around to find Nick standing behind her. All her senses leaped to awareness, and she stared at him. She noted the way the navy T-shirt he wore under his open denim jacket stretched across his chest. His jeans clung to his thighs. Suddenly, she wished she was wearing something other than her usual much washed and still dirt-stained jeans, pilled sweater, and sweatsuit jacket. The men's construction boots on her feet only added to her less-than-appealing image. At least her bright red work gloves were in her jacket pocket for the moment.

Realizing what she was doing, she forced her gaze to his. Her wayward blood throbbed. Why, she wondered dimly, did he have to look so good? She reminded herself of the destruction she'd caused in the past, and the harsh rule she had to live by. Nick Mikaris was strictly off limits.

"Good morning," she croaked. She cleared her throat. "Good morning, Mr. Mikaris."

"Nick."

She felt Duane and Roger scrutinize her closely. Her face heated. She was positive she'd be in for a lot of ribbing from them.

"Nick," she repeated, hoping her smile would cover the blush. "We were just discussing exactly what would suit the farmhouse."

She introduced Duane and Roger to him, and sensed a strange tension on Nick's part. But as he shook hands, she decided she must be imagining things.

"We'll be finished with the exterior by the end of the week," Nick said.

She nodded. "You mentioned that yesterday. We can bring in the backhoe then, and start the general contouring."

"Fine. I want this model to seem to be someone's home." He gave her a curious look. "I was thinking of knocking down some of the trees in the back and putting in a tennis court to show the possibilities of the property. But I'd have to fence the court in, and that's unsightly. Do you think you can do something with it?"

"That shouldn't be a problem," Jess lied, panic-stricken at the thought of an ugly fenced-in tennis court, let alone trying to beautify the thing. She wanted to make this a real English countryside setting, and it would take a thousand evergreens to hide the court. She didn't have time to fool around with a thousand evergreens. "However, what we were thinking of was doing one of those beautiful sweeping back lawns, with a large fountain display as a centerpiece."

"It'll be right off the back terrace," Roger chimed in.

"Back terrace?" Nick repeated in obvious confusion. "I hadn't planned on a terrace."

"You haven't?" Jess exclaimed, raising her eyebrows in mock surprise. Bless Roger for coming up with a terrace. "But a terrace would be gorgeous. There's about three acres back there, right?" Nick nodded, and she continued, "The various things that could be done with it are tremendous. But not every potential buyer will want a tennis court, or stables, or a pool, let's say. But if it's on the model property, they'll psychologically think that they'll be stuck with one. It's better, maybe, to show the buyer an English home in as natural a setting as possible, then discuss the customizing that they want for their own place."

"It will look like a lot of lawn to mow," Nick said dubiously.

"It will look like a good deal of property for the money, and the kind of people who can afford the place aren't going to be mowing their own lawns. Put in the back terrace, and let us do the rest."

He smiled wryly. "And if I insist on the tennis court?"

"Then we'll work with it." She could almost hear the groans from Duane and Roger. "But it won't be nearly as eye-catching as a fountain display."

"Then do the fountain." He glanced at her employees. "I've had the contract drawn up. It's in the trailer."

"Fine."

She walked with him to the trailer, all the while conscious of his body so close to hers. Being around him yesterday had been distracting enough. Today was worse. Men and women worked together all the time, she told herself. She could handle this. She was a professional.

He opened the door of the trailer and she stepped inside. He joined her. The door shut behind him.

Jess swallowed back butterflies at the realization that they were alone. Okay, so she was very attracted to him, but she could control it. She had to.

"Here it is," he said, picking some papers off his

desk. "Three copies. One for you, one for me, and one for Marty as the firm's lawyer."

"May I?"

She indicated a chair by the desk, and he nodded. She sat down, removed her jacket, and began to read the contract carefully. Or tried to. Her mind was totally distracted by his presence. Finally she settled for skimming through it. Everything seemed in order, including the terms of their bet. Taking up a pen, she signed the three copies.

"That was quick," Nick said, frowning at her.

"I'm a speed reader."

"Shouldn't you have your lawyer check it?"

"He drew it up. Marty Fitzgerald is my lawyer, too."

He smiled. "I forgot. His wife is one of your friends, right?"

She nodded and handed the contracts back to him. He leaned over her closely in order to sign them at the desk. As she watched him sign each copy, she could smell the scent of newly cut wood. And she smelled male. Expensive cologne couldn't excite the senses more, she thought. If she wanted, she could reach out and touch his cheek. Even though he was cleanly shaven, he possessed just a hint of beard. It would be slightly rough under her fingers . . . her lips . . . .

"Well, I'll get back to work," she muttered, and scooted out of the trailer.

When the door slammed shut behind her, she breathed a huge sigh of relief. Another moment alone with him, and she probably would have kissed him.

Gritting her teeth, she decided she'd have to avoid Nick Mikaris like the plague.

* * *

Alone, Nick cursed as he looked at the signatures on the contracts. Why had he ever insisted on a strictly business relationship with her? He had barely been able to keep from kissing her soft lips. Her smile went right through him. And her legs . . . Those worn jeans of hers clung to their smooth length, driving him wild.

Stupid, Mikaris, he thought. He had known since yesterday that working with her was the last thing he wanted. He should have told her to forget the job. Then he should have asked her to dinner. But a dumb practical joke compounded by an injury to his pride had prevented that sensible course of action.

He admitted the idea of a personal relationship with Jess was exciting. More than exciting. It could easily become an obsession. His night had been haunted by the apparition of her, clad in a sexy slip . . . and then nothing. She had something about her, something that drew him to her. He wanted her, wanted to feel her beneath him . . . .

He thought of her two employees. Where the hell had she found them? Duane and Roger were young, well-built, handsome blonds. They would put his brother to shame for size and looks. He had disliked them on sight, and liked even less the easy smiles they exchanged with Jess. He told himself they were probably idiots, but he knew the thought of her working closely with them had spurred him to give her a hard time about a tennis court he'd never intended to build in the first place. Maybe he'd labeled the wrong people idiots.

He had to stop acting like an adolescent boy desperate to get a girl's attention. He was a man.

The door to the trailer suddenly swung open. He glanced up to find Jess standing on the threshold.

"I'm sorry to disturb you, but I forgot my copy of the contract," she said.

He held it out. She stepped forward to take it from him and her fingers accidentally touched his.

She glanced up at him, her eyes wide with emotion.

He stared at her, watching the faintest of blushes color her cheeks.

Her gaze focused on his mouth.

"Hell," he muttered.

"Damn," she whispered.

He pulled her to him and settled his lips firmly on hers.

Four

His kiss was that of a man who knew what made the heart race and the blood throb. It seduced with pleasure, and yet left her wanting more—much more.

For a long moment, Jess instinctively responded to the wildfire his mouth created. Then she realized what she was doing, and scrambled out of his arms.

"I'm sorry," she mumbled, horrified by her lack of control. "That was . . . it wasn't proper."

"I will admit," Nick said, "that it was inevitable."

No, she thought. It was impossible. She lifted her chin. "It won't happen again."

The word "liar" screamed across her brain. She ignored it.

She picked up her copy of the contract. "I'll leave you to your work."

She turned around and walked out of the trailer.

The next morning, Jess jammed her sun hat on

and paced off the outer border of the front garden. A stream of measuring tape followed behind her.

"Stake it here, Duane," she called out. She stuffed her gloves in a pocket and wrote the final footage on her sketchbook. She smiled. The area was even more than she'd thought. She knew she could do a lot with it. She turned around to tell Duane to let go of the other end of the tape, but the words died in her throat.

Nick was striding across the drive toward the office trailer.

Swallowing, Jess whipped back around and yelled, "I think I'll go in back and measure out the terrace."

Trying to keep her composure, she walked as sedately as possible to the side of the large farmhouse. When she figured she was out of sight of the front, she finished the distance with a speed an Olympic sprinter would have admired.

Once she turned the back corner, she breathed a heavy sigh of relief and berated herself at the same time. She knew running like that had been an act of self-preservation. She'd bumped into Nick once earlier today, and after good mornings had been exchanged, she had found herself staring at his mouth. Years of self-control had been wiped away with one kiss.

The truth was, the kiss had stirred something inside her, something long dormant. In spite of all her efforts to blank it out, her brain had insisted on replaying the incident again and again. She'd come out of several daydreams to find her fingers caressing her lips. She swallowed heavily. She was afraid to be around him. And if she were alone with him . . .

Oh, Lord, Jess thought, closing her eyes. He hadn't fired her for her first lapse of professional behavior, and she was grateful for that. But he'd never tolerate another. And if he did . . . she dreaded the consequences. She lost her control around this man. She sensed that after she ruined everything, as she always did, she'd suffer more than guilt this time—much more.

Composing herself, Jess opened her eyes, only to see the unwound end of the measuring tape snaking past the side of the house.

"Hell's bells," she muttered.

She tiptoed over to the corner and peeked around the side. Sure enough, there was a long trail of bright yellow tape. Fortunately, Duane wasn't on the other end of it. She must have pulled it right out of his hands when she'd made her escape.

Frantically cranking the little rewinding mechanism, she prayed Duane wouldn't say anything about it.

A short time later, she discovered she wasn't quite so lucky.

"Jess wants to know what size you're planning for the terrace."

Standing in the model's kitchen, Nick sourly eyed the bearer of this request. Yesterday's dislike of Roger had strangely intensified. It was irrational, he thought in disgust. But dammit! The kid looked twice as healthy today.

"Whatever she wants is fine," he said gruffly.

"Maybe you ought to come outside and talk to her about it," Roger suggested, smiling.

That was the last thing Nick wanted to do. Being alone with Jess Brannen was like being in heaven and hell at the same time. He would want, need, to taste that incredible mouth again. And if he did, he'd make a total fool of himself.

"I've got a lot of work to do in here." He waved a hand at the half finished oak-and-glass kitchen cabinets. They were a decent excuse. "The outside is her responsibility, so the size of the terrace is her decision. I'll put in whatever she thinks is best."

Roger shrugged and disappeared out the Dutch door.

Nick grimaced. While it seemed silly, he knew the best solution to his attraction to Jess Brannen was to avoid her altogether. After his lecture to her about being a professional, he'd been the one to act unprofessionally. And at the first opportunity. Worse, in a moment of vulnerability he'd tried to excuse the kiss as something he had needed to get out of his system.

After she had run out of the trailer, he'd realized the trailer door had been wide open when he kissed her. But when he looked outside, nobody seemed interested in the trailer or its occupants. At least, they had both been spared that embarrassment.

Fortunately, she'd left shortly afterward with her employees, Hulk One and Hulk Two. But out of sight was hardly out of mind, and it had taken all his willpower to suppress the delicious lingering sensations of the kiss for the rest of the day. The night, however, had been a different story.

Just knowing she was on the site was an irresistible temptation. She had made it very clear, too, that the kiss would not be repeated. And that only made the thought of it even more addicting.

But how, he wondered, could he possibly ignore her, especially with that crazy hat she was wearing? He'd been totally disconcerted earlier by her beautiful face under a hat emblazoned with the logo *Burns Root Rot*. Between that and the bright red gloves she wore, he hadn't been able to stammer more than a terse "Good morning" to her. One good thing about the hat, he thought. It had saved him from a repeat performance of yesterday.

Still, he told himself, it was best if he had as little physical and visual contact with her as possible. Convincing himself to follow through on that, however, was another matter.

She'd just better keep wearing that hat.

During lunch, Jess finally gave in to a curiosity that had niggled at her since she'd first seen the model house. When lunch break was called, everyone left the house, including Nick. If she wanted a look at the inside—and she did—now was her chance.

As she approached the door, she gripped her portfolio more tightly and told herself she needed to see the interior, just to make sure they hadn't done something outlandishly modern with it. She hoped not. She'd once been asked to landscape a beautiful eighteenth-century Georgian brick home in West Chester, only to discover the owners had had the inside completely redone in ultramodern. She shuddered, remembering the low Danish settees and the horrible geometric mobile hanging from the out-of-place cathedral ceiling. She'd refused the job on the spot.

"What a desecration that was," she muttered.

Slipping inside, she smiled with pleasure at the sight of the long front hall. The pristine white plaster walls were interspersed at regular intervals with heavy dark timbers. Smaller timbers were angled between the larger ones as if bracing the walls. Halfway down the hall a narrow staircase led to the upper floor, and doors closed off each of the rooms from the hall. The plywood subflooring had yet to be covered.

A stone floor would make the hall perfect, she instantly decided. If it were her home, she'd decorate the hall with little tables—two, maybe three—and have vases of fresh flowers sitting atop them. Several Rubens prints hanging from the walls would give it that final old-world touch.

As she began to explore the rest of the downstairs, she was delighted with what she saw. Although the walls were bare of any covering and the floors hadn't been finished, she could easily envision each room done in an elegant sparseness, giving the impression of graciousness and space. Clutter would be a disaster. Nick had done so well with the house that it would look no different if it were set next to a real four-hundred-year-old Elizabethan manor in the Cotswolds.

When she came upon a tiny powder room hidden behind the stairs, she couldn't help grinning as she stepped inside. It reminded her of a water closet she'd seen on a tour of Windsor Castle in England. Even this was perfect.

A cough startled her, and she whirled around to

discover Nick standing on the threshold. His gaze bore into hers, and she was all too aware that she was alone in the house with him. So much for trying to avoid him, she thought frantically.

"Is the plumbing connected?" she asked.

"No."

"Fine. I'll test it anyway."

She shut the door in his face. Leaning weakly against the wood, she breathed a sign of relief. To her surprise, a burst of genuine laughter came from the other side. It was the first time she'd ever heard Nick Mikaris laugh, and she liked the sound of it.

"How's the plumbing?" he asked, still laughing.

She grinned, relaxing now that there was a stout barrier of wood between them. "Fine, just fine. And it's so silent, too."

"I aim to please. Are you pleased, Jess?"

She decided she'd only imagined a sexy drawl in his tone. "Very."

"Good. Do you always hang around in bathrooms?"

"They're nice little rooms. Why don't you try one of the other ones in the house? I'm sure you'll like it."

"No, thanks. I have this thing about hanging around just outside closed bathroom doors."

"I think we're sick people, Nick."

"I prefer depraved. Would you care for a *Reader's Digest*? I believe that's required reading for bathrooms."

"Thank you, but no." What she really needed was the Sunday edition of *The New York Times*. That took forever to read, and she had a feeling she was going to be in here forever.

"Ah . . . Nick?"

"Yes?"

"Could you go away?"

"I don't think so."

"You're missing lunch."

"I need to lose a few pounds."

"I think I hear the phone ringing in the office trailer."

"The answering machine will pick it up. Are you planning to come out anytime in the near future?"

"Why? Do you need to use the facilities?"

He started laughing again. Jess realized it wasn't the sound she liked. It was him. She closed her eyes. She didn't want to like him. Not that. Please, not that.

"You're not coming out, are you?"

"I told you I like bathrooms. Just pass a sandwich under the door every so often and I'll be fine. I prefer tuna with lettuce and tomato."

There was no answer from the other side.

"Nick?" she asked, frowning at the unexpected silence. She set her portfolio down next to the vanity.

"Nick? Nick?"

When she still didn't receive an answer, she pressed her ear to the door. She didn't hear anything, but that didn't necessarily mean he wasn't there. After another minute, she found enough courage to crack open the door and peek outside.

He was gone.

"Well, hell," she muttered, opening the door wider and stepping out into the empty hall. She wasn't sure whether she was grateful or angry for his sudden disappearance.

She chuckled as she remembered her last remark. Maybe he'd gone to get her a sandwich. Then she sighed.

She'd forgotten to tell him she liked her tuna on rye.

Nick riffled through the blueprints spread out on the butcher-block kitchen counter and pulled one from the bottom.

"This is it, Sam," he said, handing it to his foreman.

"Thanks."

Once Sam left, Nick hurried back to the powder room. To his disappointment, the door was wide open and the room was empty.

Damn, he thought. While Jess had been saying something about slipping a sandwich under the door, Sam had signaled him from the kitchen end of the hall. He hadn't wanted his foreman to know he and Jess had been talking through a closed bathroom door, so he'd simply slipped away quietly. Although he had only been gone a short time, it had obviously been long enough for her to come out.

She was something, he thought, smiling as he continued down the hall to the stairs. She had shut that bathroom door in his face with great dignity, and he hadn't been able to resist teasing her while she was inside. In fact, he'd been enjoying himself so much that he'd resented Sam's interruption.

But it was probably just as well. The lunch break was almost over and very shortly the men would be back inside the house. And he'd better check on the progress of the upstairs rooms before they started. He'd noticed earlier that the sky was starting to cloud over, and although the weather report called for rain in the evening, he had a feeling it would start a good deal sooner than that. If it did, he hoped he had enough inside work for all the men. Otherwise they'd get the rest of the day off with pay. He was already cutting it too close to the budget as it was.

Once he reached the upper floor, he walked directly into the master bedroom. It was nearly finished. Hell, he thought. The budget might be a little tight, but the work was actually ahead of schedule. Still, he'd find something for his men to do.

Light footsteps in the hall caught his attention. He glanced around just in time to see Jess walk into the room. She was gazing upward, obviously taking in the ten-foot bedroom ceiling. The instant she lowered her head she spotted him, and her feet faltered.

"It's my turn," he said, holding up a hand. As he walked toward the master bathroom, he added, "I prefer roast beef. Hold the mayo."

He shut the bathroom door.

She burst into laughter.

Later that night, Jess was still smiling when she emerged from her shower. She just couldn't help it. She wanted to laugh every time she thought of Nick strolling into the master bathroom like that. She was tempted to bring him a roast beef sandwich tomorrow, no mayo, just in case he wanted to hang out at "their" spot.

Her amusement subsided, though, as she dried herself off and put on her nightgown and quilted robe. She picked up a comb and slowly began to untangle her wet hair. She never would have imagined that Nick Mikaris had a playful side. After what had happened at the hotel, she'd been sure the man was completely lacking a sense of humor about anything. But he'd teased her today. She couldn't remember the last time a man had made her laugh.

Abruptly, she realized she was allowing herself to daydream about a normal relationship with Nick. Daydreams opened the way for reality. Destructive reality. A normal relationship wasn't for her. It wasn't that she blamed the entire male species for the actions of one. A long time ago she'd understood that was silly. But the divorce had had unexpected ramifications. The truth was, the flaw was within herself.

She cringed, as she remembered being trapped behind that bathroom door. How silly would she get in her desperation to avoid Nick?

"Don't answer that," she muttered in disgust. "You really don't want to know."

The more she was determined to act like the adult she was, the more she acted like a twelve-year-old. She'd never done this kind of thing even when she had been twelve! This was it, she decided. Beginning tomorrow, she'd act like a mature businesswoman. She'd do her sketches tonight, and in the morning she'd sit down with Nick and discuss her plans for the property. She had a job to do, and she damn well better start doing it.

"Hell!" she exclaimed, realizing that she hadn't walked into her house with her portfolio. In fact, the last time she remembered having it was when she'd been exploring the model house. Obviously, she'd been more rattled than she'd thought since she'd never forgotten her portfolio before. The sketches would have to wait until tomorrow morning.

Her doorbell rang just then, and she hurried to answer it.

She put her eye to the peephole and was shocked to see Tony Mikaris on her doorstep. What was he doing here? she wondered, and opened the door.

"I'm Tony Mikaris, Ms. Brannen," the young man said. He had a defiant look in his eyes. "I don't know if you remember me or not. We . . . met in Atlantic City the other day."

"I remember," she said, giving him a cool smile. Oh brother, did she remember!

"I'm sorry to disturb you so late," he added stiffly. "But it's important that I talk to you."

"I see." Watching him turn up the collar of his bomber jacket against the steady, chilling rain, she added, "Come in."

He stepped in just far enough so that she could shut the door behind him.

"Look, I'm really sorry about the joke I played on you and my brother," he said, relaxing a little. "Sandy told me you were supposed to landscape Nick's homes, and it screwed everything up for you. I just got in from Baltimore, and I haven't seen Nick yet. When I do, I'll explain everything to him and make sure he doesn't blame you. I wanted to apologize to you first, Ms. Brannen, since you were the innocent victim of my trying to get at my brother."

As she gazed at Tony, Jess knew it couldn't have been easy for him to come here and admit his guilt. But he'd done it, and she could hardly find it in herself to be angry with him.

"Call me Jess," she said, smiling. "I should hang you by your thumbs, you know. However, your brother hired me anyway."

Tony's eyebrows seemed to shoot off his forehead. "You're kidding!"

"No, and it wasn't easy."

"I'll bet."

"That's about what it took," she murmured.

"I beg your pardon?"

"Never mind."

He shrugged. "Well, I'm glad that worked out at least, although I'm surprised you managed to get around him. He's been . . . rigid ever since his marriage."

"He's . . ." She swallowed heavily. "I didn't know he was married."

"He's divorced now."

She tried to ignore the relief that ran through her.

"That was a long time ago," Tony continued. "But he hasn't loosened up at all. And he hates my dancing."

She chuckled. "I can't imagine Nick would be the kind of person who'd stand up and cheer."

Tony made a face. "Trust me, he's not. It's been a continual argument ever since I started. That was the reason I pulled the joke in the first place. I knew I was going to get another lecture from him, and I thought that if he were caught with his pants down, figuratively speaking, maybe he'd take a good hard look at himself and realize what he's been like. Maybe he'd even start to relax a little. But I expected to find you there when I walked him up to his room that night. Where did you disappear to at two A.M.? I was in the room when your friends put you in there, and you were flat out."

"That's probably when I was in the bathroom exorcising the Bahama Mamas I drank." Jess shuddered. "I will never touch those things again. They're lethal."

"Well, I'm glad I didn't ruin the job for you," he said, putting his hand on the doorknob. "Again, I'm really sorry about what hap—"

The ringing of the doorbell interrupted him.

"Great," Jess muttered. It figured that the whole world would drop in for a visit when she was in her "jammies." Brushing past Tony, she glanced through the peephole. Disaster stood on her doorstep.

"It's Nick!"

Five

"Nick!" Tony exclaimed in astonishment.

His voice seemed to reverberate through the house, and Jess clamped a hand over his mouth. She could easily imagine Nick's reaction to finding his handsome, single brother here—especially with the way she was dressed. She didn't even want to attempt explaining her way out of this one.

The doorbell rang again.

"Just a minute!" she shouted.

She dragged Tony away from the door and into the living room. "Be quiet!" she whispered. "I don't want Nick to know that you're here."

Tony pulled her hand away. "But—"

She practically slammed her hand over his mouth this time. "Will you keep your voice down!"

"Mmmpff!" Tony twisted his head away and asked in a low voice, "Jess, what's all the fuss about?"

"Your brother thinks I'm the original fun-time girl. Lord knows what he'll think when he sees you here, and I can't afford that. Damn! Where can I hide you?" Her downstairs consisted of a living room/dining room combination with the kitchen separated from it by a counter bar. A powder room was situated to the left of the counter area.

"Get in the bathroom." She shoved Tony toward it as the doorbell rang a third time. "I'm coming!"

"Look, I'll explain everything to Nick," Tony said, resisting her efforts to hustle him into the bathroom. "It will be awkward at first—"

"Awkward is when one is caught with a surprise visitor while fully dressed. My attire is a different cupcake, Tony."

"You've got a point," he conceded.

"Good. Now just be a nice guy and get in the damn bathroom until I get rid of him."

"I've heard of women hiding men in closets, but not bathrooms," Tony said, finally cooperating with her.

"Bathrooms are turning out to be my specialty." She pushed him into the little room. "Don't move until I come and get you. And don't you ever breathe a word of this to anybody!"

As soon as she shut the bathroom door on Tony, she whirled around and raced for the front door. She was panting for breath when she opened it. Nick smiled, her portfolio tucked under his arm. The rain had started in earnest again, and he was sopping wet.

"Nick!" she exclaimed. "Come in, come in."

She sent a desperate prayer toward the bathroom for its occupant not even to breathe, let alone sneeze.

Nick stepped inside, and she shut the door behind him.

"I thought you might need this," he said, holding the portfolio out to her.

"It was very thoughtful of you to bring it to me." She took the portfolio from him, wishing he hadn't picked this particular night to be so gentlemanly. One courtly Mikaris at a time was quite enough. Forcing a smile, she added, "The rain came so quickly that we had to race for the trucks, and I didn't even realize I'd left my sketches behind until a few minutes ago. I hope you haven't gone too far out of your way to return this."

"No." He glanced around. Jess held her breath. He looked back at her, surveying her attire. "I've come at a bad time, haven't I?"

"Oh . . . ah . . . well, I'd just gotten out of the shower when the doorbell rang." She set the portfolio down on the table in the entryway, then pushed her damp hair behind her shoulder and clutched her robe to her throat. "Really, though, it's no problem. I'm only sorry I kept you waiting so long."

"But . . ." He looked puzzled. "I could have sworn I heard voices."

"Voices!" she squeaked, panic running through her. Obviously, she and Tony hadn't been as quiet as she'd hoped. Thinking fast, she said, "It must have been the television you heard. I turned it off right before I answered the door."

"You leave the television on when you're in the shower?"

"Ahh . . . I'm a TV freak. Yes, that's it. I leave it on all the time." Desperate to change the subject to anything but voices, she said, "It must be really pouring out there. You're all wet, Nick."

He chuckled. "Yes, I know. Could I borrow your bathroom?"

"My bathroom!" she exclaimed in shock. "What do you want the bathroom for? I mean . . . well, it's a mess right now. A real mess. Sorry I snapped, but I just didn't expect you to ask to use the bathroom."

He grinned. "I don't care what it looks like, Jess. I only wanted a towel to dry off before I go back out in the rain again."

"Oh, of course." She smiled brightly and said in a very loud voice, "Let me get you a towel, Nick. It must really be pouring out there. You're soaking wet."

"So you told me," he murmured, shrugging out of his leather jacket.

Nodding, she took it from him and dropped it over the back of the sofa, then hurried to the powder room. She had no sooner opened the door when a hand thrust a towel at her. She grabbed it and rushed back to Nick.

"Here you go. A nice dry towel."

"Thanks."

As he began to rub the excess water from his hair, she sighed inwardly. She'd been a towel away from total disaster.

"It was really nice of you to bring me my portfolio," she said. "And on such a miserable night."

"I was glad to do it," he said from under the towel. She heard him yawn. "Lord, but I'm bushed."

Horrified that he might ask to borrow a bed, she said, "How about some coffee? I bet you'd love a cup of coffee right now."

He flipped the towel up and smiled at her. "I wouldn't say no."

"Wonderful!" she exclaimed. "I'll have it ready in a jiffy."

She raced into the kitchen and literally threw coffee and water into the brewer. As she switched it on, realization dawned. She was stuck with him through a cup of coffee. If she had only remained calm, she could have been sending him on his way by now.

"Damn," she muttered, deciding against fixing a plate of cookies too. Courtesy only went so far. Hoping Tony would hear her, she bellowed, "Two minutes, and you can have a nice *quick* cup of coffee, Nick!"

"I'm right here," he said from behind her.

She whipped around to find him sitting on one of the stools on the other side of the counter. "I'm sorry, I didn't hear you."

She swallowed at the dazzling smile he gave her.

"I was really sorry the rain started right after lunch today," she went on, leaning against the stove. "I had been hoping to get the back part of the property roughed out this afternoon."

He shrugged. "It's supposed to clear up tomorrow. I was lucky to find enough work inside for the men."

Recognizing she had a nice neutral topic at hand, Jess nodded eagerly. "The weather's a real problem for construction and landscaping, isn't it? Especially landscaping. You can't work outdoors in the winter. Well, you can in certain instances. And then you have the spring rains to contend with. Summer kills everything with the heat. And with the fall, you've got balmy skies one day and frost the next . . ."

She was babbling, and she knew it. Fortunately, she was saved by the last sputter of the coffee maker.

"Coffee's ready," she said, and hurried over to a cabinet.

As she reached up to get a cup hanging from a cupboard hook, her arm brushed the one next to it. It fell off the hook with a clatter, and she scrambled to catch it as it rolled toward the edge of the shelf.

"Very good," Nick said.

"Thanks," she said, glancing over her shoulder at him as she set the cup down on the counter.

But the near miss with the cup seemed to turn her into a klutz. She fumbled with the saucers and it took three tries before her suddenly shaking hands could get two spoons out of the silverware drawer. The sugar bowl was nearly empty, and she spilled more fresh sugar on the counter top than she managed to get into the bowl.

Brushing the crystals aside, she sighed in exasperation. She had good reason to be nervous, she thought. But not this nervous. Pulling herself together, she opened the refrigerator door. She was determined to get out the half-and-half without incident.

Two seconds later, she helplessly gazed at the creamer shattered on the floor in front of her refrigerator.

"I think I'd better pour the coffee," Nick said, coming up behind her.

"Smart man."

After cleaning up the mess, she joined Nick at the counter, and, to her surprise, actually spooned sugar and cream into her cup without mishap. She took a sip . . . and gagged on the mud she'd created.

"This is awful," she pronounced in disgust.

Nick grinned. "It's hot. And it probably has enough caffeine to keep me awake for the next three days."

She opened her mouth to say she'd make another pot, then shut it. She wasn't that dumb. Besides, she'd probably dump coffee all over the kitchen this time. She took another sip. It really wasn't that bad—if one liked hot mud.

Her facial expression must have betrayed something of her thoughts, because Nick reached over and covered her hand with his.

"Jess, the coffee's just fine."

His touch coursed through her veins, nearly toppling what little control she had. She pulled her hand away, picked up her cup, and took a big gulp of coffee.

"You know, you're right. The coffee's just fine," she said in a rush, hoping to hide her abrupt breaking of physical contact. "So who do you follow in the sports world, Nick? The Eagles? Flyers? It's baseball season, isn't it? You probably follow the Phillies. Everyone does. So what do you think? Will Mike Schmidt's legs hold out for another season? Astroturf has ruined more ball players—"

His burst of laughter interrupted her rapid-fire monologue.

"What's so funny?" she asked, glaring at him.

"You. First you're not sure if it is baseball season, then you're asking me about Mike Schmidt's legs."

"I just forgot it was spring," she retorted.

She definitely wasn't cut out to hide a man in her bathroom with aplomb, she thought. She knew she had overreacted about Tony's presence. Maybe she hadn't made the best of first impressions with Nick, but he seemed to be overlooking that. Despite her internal lectures, she continued to make a fool of herself around him. Now she was stuck. This was the last time, she vowed.

"Schmitty's legs will be fine," Nick said, breaking into her thoughts. "But I'd rather talk about you. I have to admit that I thought you'd live in a mansion."

She shook her head. "Actually, I've never lived in a mansion. My parents had an apartment."

"You're kidding!"

She smiled wryly. "Well, I will admit it was a penthouse. But an apartment is an apartment."

"Any brothers or sisters?"

"I'm it. My father likes to say I was more than enough."

"And you're single."

"Divorced. Same as you."

"How do you know I'm divorced?" he asked, surprise evident in his voice. "I know I never told you that."

"Sandy mentioned it," she lied, trying to look as innocent as possible.

"Oh." He seemed to relax. "What's the state of your love life now? Other than our kiss, of course."

A thump came from the bathroom, as if in answer. Jess froze.

"What was that?" Nick asked.

"Oh . . . the cat. It must be my cat. I have a cat." She prayed he believed her, even while she was horrified at how fast she was lying to this man.

"In the bathroom?"

"He likes the bathroom." She giggled nervously. "Just like me. He's afraid of people, so he hides whenever anybody comes to the house. He's a funny little thing. I've had him for two years, and even my parents have yet to see anything other than a blur diving under the sofa."

"The door's shut."

"What?"

He pointed toward the powder room. "The door's shut. How did he shut the door behind him?"

"Damn!" She decided to brazen her way out of this disaster. Hurrying around the counter bar, she said, "Who knows with cats. He must have bumped it somehow, racing in there when he heard you ring the doorbell. Once he jumped in the hamper and the lid swung shut on him."

"What's his name?"

"Cat."

"That's it? Just Cat?"

"I have no imagination when it comes to names." She cracked the door open a bare inch. "Here, Cat . . . psss, psss. Come on, Cat. Nick won't hurt you."

Complete astonishment shot clear down to her toes when a piteous "meow" came from inside the powder room. It sounded exactly like a frightened cat.

Finally taking a deep breath to calm herself, she turned around and shrugged. "He's not a very bright cat. I'll just leave the door cracked open for him."

Nick nodded, then drained the last of the coffee from his cup. He looked at her expectantly.

She smiled. "I'm sorry the coffee wasn't the best. You look really tired, Nick. I'm sure you want to get home."

The last thing he looked was tired, but she hoped he'd get the hint.

He rose from the bar stool. "That's me. Wet and tired. Thanks for the coffee and the towel."

"You're welcome."

She walked with him to the door. He retrieved his jacket from the back of the sofa. As he put it on, she opened the door. He turned to face her.

She gazed up at him, then realized that was exactly what she'd done before she'd kissed him yesterday. Instantly, she looked away.

Clearing her throat, she said, "Thank you for bringing me my portfolio."

"You're very welcome."

He traced her jawline with a gentle finger, then strode out the door.

It took Jess a full minute to come to her senses. Closing the door, she leaned against it and sighed loudly. What a night! Nick Mikaris was complicating her life—in every way.

But now, she had to get his brother out of the bathroom.

She walked into the center of the living room.

"Ollie, ollie, all's in free!"

Parked two doors down and across the street from Jess's townhouse, Nick sat in his darkened car and chuckled over Mike Schmidt's legs. That unexpected little gem coming from Jess Brannen's mouth had been astonishing.

He was glad now he'd found her portfolio and decided to return it. The truth was, he hadn't been able *not* to come by, although when he first heard voices he'd very much wished otherwise—especially when she'd answered the door in her robe. Her odd nervousness had thrown him, too, and then he'd seen the closed door off the kitchen. He could still feel the hard anger that had curled through him. But the cat had cried out, and he'd realized he was being ridiculous in thinking Jess would hide someone there. He'd never considered that she might have a lover, and he reluctantly admitted she had no reason to hide one from him. He had no claim on her . . . .

Nick fumed. He'd been the one to insist on a strictly business relationship, even knowing Jess inspired in him a desire for something entirely different. She was soft and sexy, poised and elegant. He sensed that in the bedroom, she would drive a man to the brink of insanity. Seeing her dressed in a nightgown and robe, her hair gleaming damply around her shoulders, he had nearly gone crazy himself. The only thing that had kept him in control was the realization that she was nervous about being alone with him. He'd found it endearing.

Jess Brannen made him laugh—a lot. He felt young and carefree, as if he didn't have a responsibility in the world. No one had ever made him feel that way before.

From the first moment they'd met, he hadn't been at all fair to her. Part of it had been his humiliation at her innocent hands in that hotel room. So she had had a mistaken impression of his sexual preference. He finally admitted the other part of his problem had been her background. He was wealthy in his own right, although his money was tied up completely in his business. But he was proud of it. He'd earned it through a great deal of hard work and sacrifice.

Starting tomorrow, he vowed, his relationship with Jess would be entirely different.

Glancing over at her house, he wondered what she would think about the brand-new Nick Mi—

Her front door opened and Tony emerged into the light of the porch lamp.

Nick watched numbly as his brother turned up the collar of his jacket and hurried down the sidewalk in the opposite direction.

Suddenly, he felt a hundred years old.

Six

Nick walked into his house to discover his brother seated on the couch watching television, a can of beer in his hand. Nick had taken a long drive to cool his anger, but the sight of Tony making himself at home brought it all back again.

"Hi," Tony said. "Just thought I'd stop in and—"

"Did you and Jess have a good laugh after I left?" Nick asked caustically, cutting off his brother's greeting.

Tony stared at him in clear amazement. "What!"

"Don't play innocent," Nick said between clenched teeth. He should have known Jess Brannen wasn't quite what she seemed. "I know you were at her place tonight. Probably upstairs in her bed. I'm not as stupid as you like to think I am, little brother. Or as stupid as you are. She's playing you for a fool, Tony. I know, because she's trying to play me for one."

"Are you finished?"

"Damn straight I am."

"Good," Tony said calmly. "I'm not sixteen, Nick. And she's not Janet."

Nick's anger died instantly at the mention of his ex-wife. "That incident never once came to mind, Tony."

"I'm glad to hear that." Tony stood up and walked over to him. "Jess Brannen is a nice woman. She wouldn't try to seduce her husband's brother, and she wouldn't run her husband into debt for thousands either. Janet was a bitch from the first. It just took you a little while to see it."

"I know." Nick took a deep breath and slowly let it out. He remembered all too well when Tony had run away shortly after moving into Nick and Janet's home, after their mother had died. It had taken three days to find him, and about two minutes to discover that Janet had been trying to get a mixed-up, grieving sixteen-year-old into her bed. The only thing Janet had succeeded in was finally showing her true self.

Still, that didn't explain to Nick why he'd seen Tony coming out of Jess's house right after him. But it was him Jess had kissed in the office trailer, not Tony. That needed some explaining, too, and he braced himself for the worst. Tony had never lied to him, but Nick knew he'd prefer a lie right now to hearing that his brother and Jess had an intimate relationship.

"So why were you at her house tonight?" he asked, as calmly as possible.

"That's none of your business," Tony said flatly. "But I'm going to be nice about it. Before you condemn us to the gallows, you might like to know that I only saw Jess to apologize about the practical joke. I didn't know that she had this landscaping thing going on with you. When I heard about it from Sandy, I knew I might have made things difficult for her with the job. That's the only reason I went to see her."

"That doesn't explain why I didn't see you inside the house."

"You no sooner knocked on the door, when she started shoving me toward the nearest hidey-hole while babbling something about your thinking she's the 'original fun-time girl.'" Tony shook his head. "She didn't think you'd believe I was there for an entirely innocent reason. I thought you would. Obviously, you really are more stupid than I think you are."

Nick tried to digest the information. "You mean, she didn't want me to see you because I might think you were there for more than an apology?"

"Which you thought. Admit it. After I saw her, I came here, as I'd originally planned to do before going back to Columbia, to insure that you wouldn't hold against her that damn joke I wish I never pulled. Dammit, Nick! She's a terrific lady."

Nick sank down into the nearest chair. Tony, knowing he'd been caught, would be crazy to try to hide anything about Jess now. It was easier for Nick to believe the worst, but he found himself accepting Tony's story. Even as a kid, Tony had usually owned up to misbehavior, sometimes before anyone had even been aware of it.

"You're right, Tony. She is a terrific lady."

Tony returned to the couch and sat down. "But that hasn't stopped you from jumping to other conclusions about her the first chance you get. So are you finally calm and straight on this? Or should I get out the dueling pistols?"

"I'm straight," Nick muttered, disgusted with himself. "But what was I supposed to think when I saw you coming out of her house like that?"

"Well, now." Tony made a show of stroking his jaw. "It isn't the perceived purpose of the visit that's so interesting. It's the reaction. Most people would just say, 'Lucky fellow, that Mikaris.' But if one has a certain affection for the lady in question, seeing another man coming out of her house would provoke an entirely different response. From tonight's evidence, my older but not necessarily wiser brother, I would say the jury's in. You've got it bad for Jessica Brannen."

"I don't know about that," Nick said, in automatic defense. "She's attractive, but I'm not about to turn into a wild man if that's what you're thinking."

"Really? Want to tell me about the kiss?"

"How the hell do you know about that?"

Tony grinned widely. "Meow."

Nick stared at his brother in confusion. "But . . . that was her cat."

Tony laughed. "That was me stuck in that damn bathroom. I felt like I was doing Cary Grant imitations in there. First, I'd think, 'This is dumb. Just go out there and explain,' then I'd think, 'No, this is what the lady wants, and I've caused her enough trouble already.' I was going 'round and 'round on the best thing to do when I heard you mention a kiss. I was so startled, I accidentally bumped against this hanging plant she has in there. Next thing I know, I'm a cat. Hell, I didn't know what else to do, so I meowed. It made sense at the time."

Nick looked at his brother, then flopped back and laughed helplessly. He knew he shouldn't be laughing, but the thought of Tony trapped in the bathroom playing a cat was too much. It was his own fault that he'd made an idiot of himself tonight with Tony. After the bad time he'd given Jess, it was no wonder she'd been uncomfortable about Tony's being in her house. It wasn't fair to her, he thought, to be enjoying what must have been a bad moment for her. It really wasn't.

"It could only happen with Jess," he said, his laughter growing when he thought of her bravura performance. "I must have scared the wits out of her when I asked to use the bathroom."

"I won't tell you what you nearly scared out of me!" Tony exclaimed, laughing with him.

"I can imagine," Nick said, wiping tears from his eyes. "Poor Jess. We really shouldn't be laughing. It isn't fair."

They gazed at each other, then doubled over again with laughter.

"So where was the cat?" Nick finally asked.

"She doesn't have one. She was so convincing that I asked about one after you left."

Nick shook his head. He thought about Atlantic City, and, despite being one of the victims of the joke, he could see the humor in it. "Her face that morning in the hotel was priceless."

"So was yours," Tony said.

"I don't doubt it."

"Especially when she thought you were gay."

"I had a tough time getting past that one with her," Nick admitted, still chuckling.

Tony smiled. "She makes you feel good, doesn't she?"

"Yes." Nick smiled back.

"So, my brother who is fooling no one, what are you going to do about Jess Brannen?"

"What do you think?"

Tony grinned.

"If you hit the house, I will personally take it out of your hide!"

Jess smiled at Nick as she climbed onto the backhoe. "It's just a little backhoe, and I've got a license to operate it. Would you like to see it?"

"No, I'd rather get your hide!"

"As long as we understand each other."

After he went into the model house, Jess slapped the earphones over her head, pulled on her red gloves, and started up the vehicle. The din, she knew, was horrendous, but fortunately the ear coverings deadened the worst of it.

Pushing controls and shifting gears, she concentrated on getting the front property contoured into its general shape.

No more hiding in bathrooms, she thought in relief. The incident with Tony and Nick last night had taken ten years off her life. This morning she had steeled herself and marched right up to Nick to tell him of her day's plans. Actually, it hadn't been too bad. In fact, he'd been quite nice, never even mentioning that he'd stopped by. And although she'd felt the pull of attraction, she had managed to dampen it to a mere ache.

She was now thinking and acting like an adult, instead of a crazy woman, she acknowledged proudly. From this day on, she'd be able to handle herself as a true profes—

Duane suddenly ran in front of the backhoe, frantically waving his arms. She stopped the machine and pulled the earphones off.

"What?" she shouted over the noise of the engine.

He pointed to her left. Glancing around, she saw that she had contoured her way past the model and onto the adjoining property. She hadn't hurt anything, but still . . .

Giving herself a mental slap, Jess backtracked the vehicle and began again. Okay, she thought, so she had a few glitches to work out.

She managed to finish the general contouring without further incident, although her mind occasionally wandered into forbidden territory. Once she was done, she turned the machine onto the dirt roadway and brought it to a halt in front of the trailer. Jumping down to the ground, she dusted her hands off and surveyed the front property. The sloping she'd created was so gradual, it was almost unnoticeable. There was only the nice deep gouge on the property next door to mar her work. Good thing the house was barely framed out, she thought. She would have had a heck of a time explaining her boo-boo to the buyers.

Somebody pulled away her earphones.

"I said, 'How about lunch?' "

Startled, she whirled around to find Nick grinning at her. "Oh! I'm sorry. I didn't hear you."

He chuckled and flicked a finger at the earphones. "I noticed. Now, for the fifth time, how about lunch?"

"I thought you needed to lose a few pounds."

He laughed. "I'm off my diet today. Besides, it will give me a chance to see those sketches you mentioned."

She found herself becoming mesmerized by his charming smile. Mentally shaking herself, she realized that the invitation was for a business discussion. That she could handle.

"I'll go get the sketches."

Ten minutes later, she was sitting in the office trailer, eating a sandwich. Although neither of them had been dressed for a restaurant, she had envisioned a McDonald's. Instead, Nick had produced a packed cooler.

"More 'wine'?" he asked, holding up a bottle of ginger ale.

She shook her head as she took a bite out of her hoagie.

"I like these very much," he said, studying the sketches. "You must have worked all night on them."

"Mmm," she said around a mouthful of tomatoes, lunch meat, bread, and onions. She swallowed. "I wanted them ready for today."

"Very professional," he murmured as she took a sip of her soda. "It's exactly how I imagined the property. You know, I think we're going to work very well together."

She immediately choked on her soda. She waved him away when he stood up to help her.

"I'm okay," she gasped. "I just swallowed wrong."

"Are you sure, Jess?" he asked, sincere concern in his eyes.

Was this, she wondered frantically, the man who, only a short week ago, was ready to throw her off the job the moment she did something out of line? Something was definitely wrong, and it wasn't her this time. Why was he being so . . . friendly? Not that he'd been mean or difficult before, she admitted.

But he had been very suspicious of her in general, and dubious of her abilities. His being nice terrified her.

"By the way, I got a little present for your cat," he said, shocking her out of her musings.

"My cat?" she echoed when she finally managed to find her voice. "You bought a present for my cat?"

"It's just a little ball stuffed with catnip," he said, handing over a small paper bag. He shrugged. "I was feeling bad that I scared him into the bathroom."

"Oh . . . ah . . . well, thank you," she said, staring at the bag. "I'm sure he'll like it."

"I've seen dogs who are scared of humans, but never a cat before. Usually, they just ignore people. Was yours abused as a kitten?"

"I've often wondered that myself," she said, groaning inwardly. "I got him from a shelter."

"Then he could have been abused as a kitten," Nick said, munching on some chips. "I would love to take the sick people who torture helpless animals and give them a little return lesson. People like that ought to be hung."

Jess wondered what her chances were of a tornado coming along and whisking her off to Oz. The man was ready to defend a nonexistent cat! Shakespeare's admonition about tangled webs and deception rang through her head. There had to be a hundred other explanations for a thump in a vacant bathroom, and she wished she'd thought of just one. Anything was better than this cat business. She felt foolish about it now, but she wasn't about to confess the truth. It was better just to slink away with a present for "Cat."

"You probably saw that I plowed over the other

property this morning," she began, hoping desperately to change the subject. "If the pile of dirt is in the men's way—"

"You plowed it over? I hadn't noticed, but I'm sure it won't be a problem. And you have to put the dirt somewhere, right?"

"Right. I've ordered the rose bushes."

"Great," Nick said enthusiastically. "I really think you've given me an excellent selling point with this authentic English rose garden. I plan to make the most of the customizing, inside and out, with buyers."

The telephone rang, halting anything further. As he answered it, she pointed toward the door, indicating that she would give him privacy. Picking up her sandwich and soda, she slipped outside.

She settled onto a small pile of cylinder bricks and admitted that she was the one who needed privacy. She just couldn't understand Nick's expansive mood today. Maybe he'd had some good news. Maybe someone had put Valium in his morning coffee.

"Nahh," she answered herself as she remembered him arguing with Sam, his foreman, first thing this morning. Nick should actually be in a bad mood for the rest of the day. She usually was when hit with problems on a job site.

She sensed, too, a subtle change in his attitude toward her. She didn't know what had happened or why, but it was there. That wasn't good. Not good at all. Although she had had a few bad times with their business relationship, it was the only relationship they could have. Knowing that, she had been safe. But now he was treating her as a friend, and she was responding. She wanted to let down barriers she'd let down before—with disastrous results. She knew herself, knew what she would eventually do. Nick Mikaris didn't deserve that.

"There you are," he said, settling down beside her. "I'm sorry about the call, but you didn't have to leave."

"It's okay," she said, edging away from him. She could feel the heat and strength emanating from his body, pulling her insides out. Attempting to keep the conversation light, she added, "Now what if it had been a supplier on the other end, demanding past due money? You certainly wouldn't want me to hear that. I might pull my firm out of the job and leave you with your dirt piled up to the eaves."

Nick grinned. "If it were a creditor, I'd already be hiding in the bathroom with your cat."

"He wouldn't let you in."

"I'd like to see him try to kick me out."

She looked away, staring at nothing.

"What's the matter, Jess?"

Her appetite gone, she wrapped up the remains of her lunch and stood up.

"Jess?"

"I like you, Nick," she said in a low voice.

"I'm glad."

"Don't be. You'll hate me in the end."

Seven

"Jess! You made it!"

"Of course, I made it," Jess said. She kissed Marty Fitzgerald on the cheek. A din of voices and laughter flowed from the living room, and she glanced inside. "The party looks like it's going strong."

"Naturally." Marty chuckled, as he helped her out of her black velvet coat, and raised his eyebrows. She was wearing a black dress whose skirt ended several inches above her knee and whose lace top gave the illusion of sheerness. "I'd leer, but I'm a happily married man."

Jess grinned. "Marty, how can someone who looks so cherubic have the heart of a lecher?"

"Ask my wife." He linked her arm through his. "Come on. I can't wait to see the eyes pop when our guests see you in that dress."

The living room was crammed with people, but she instantly spotted Sandy, who hurried over to her.

"I hope to heaven you don't have a band hiding anywhere," Sandy said, hugging her. "This is one anniversary I'd like to be nice and quiet."

"This," Jess asked, "is quiet?"

"Compared to your ideas for an anniversary celebration, it's very quiet," Sandy said tartly. She gave Marty a loving look. "Thank goodness, this was my year for the joke."

"I noticed," Jess muttered.

Sandy and Marty left her to greet more arrivals. She drifted among the guests, until she was standing alone by the mantelpiece, looking over the room. Animated conversations flowed about her, yet she found none enticing enough to join. She felt oddly out of place tonight, but she wasn't sure why. She knew a number of people in the room very well, and she always enjoyed parties. . . .

Then she caught herself searching for a face among the guests.

She was looking for Nick.

Dammit, she thought, remembering her strange eagerness when dressing for the party. She'd taken extra pains with her appearance. Had she wanted to wear something spectacular in the subconscious hope he would be here?

She had to stop this. Only this afternoon she'd been warning him off . . . and herself as well. But knowing something or someone was off limits only made the wanting stronger. It was a very human reaction, she thought. Lately, she had been having a lot of them.

"If you wanted my attention, you certainly picked the dress for it," a voice said.

She knew who had spoken even before she turned to face him.

Nick stared at the front of her dress with frank admiration. "How does it hide your . . . ah . . ."

"Prayer," she said, chuckling at his consternation. His gaze seemed to heat her skin.

"Good thing I'm an agnostic."

In his three-piece suit, white silk shirt, and elegantly knotted striped tie, he looked like he'd just stepped out of *Gentleman's Quarterly*. But then Nick's workclothes always seemed custom-made too. She almost asked when he had arrived, then realized it would sound as if she'd been waiting for him.

"Been here long?" he asked, taking her elbow. She tried to suppress her awareness of his touch as he steered her around through the crowd.

"Not too long. Where are we going?"

"To find a drink."

He was acting as if she'd never said anything out of the ordinary this afternoon, she thought. In fact, he hadn't uttered a word on the subject. She was more confused than ever. Still, she couldn't refuse a drink without looking childish, and she'd been childish enough already.

"No Bahama Mamas, please." She grinned. "The last time I had those I met you."

"I consider that an endorsement."

"I'll take a club soda anyway."

As they passed four men, one of them called out, "Who do you invest with, Mikaris?"

"John Deere," Nick replied, without stopping. "When John Deere roars, you listen."

"Nick!" she admonished, trying to choke back her laughter.

"The man asked, Jess," he said. "Besides, I really have invested a bundle in John Deere equipment. When you start up one of their tractors, you can't hear anything else."

"You are a tease," she said primly.

He grinned at her. "If we're going to talk about teasing, then let's talk about that dress."

"I think I should have worn a gunnysack."

"You'd still look great.'"

His compliment pleased her, and she knew it shouldn't. She felt as if she were playing a dangerous game. How much freedom could she give herself before the hurt came?

Or was it already too late?

By the time they reached the bar, Nick had decided Jess had deliberately worn that dress to drive him insane.

The lace on the bodice barely covered the curves of her breasts, and the tiny flounced skirt enticed the eye to her beautifully shaped legs. A diamond choker sparkled against the satiny skin of her neck. Her hair was tied back with a black bow in a simple yet chic style.

It was a delightfully shocking change from her landscaping clothes, those red gloves and that damnable hat. He hadn't been prepared for her sophistication, and he sensed the generations of breeding behind it.

Yet he had seen the depth of her vulnerability this afternoon as well. He hadn't been prepared for that either.

Setting the disturbing thought aside for the time

being, he ordered drinks from the bartender. They no sooner received them when Marty and Sandy butted between them. Nick scowled at the intrusion.

"Sandy, my love," Marty said. "Why am I under the impression that Nick is ready to strangle Jess?"

"I was under the same impression," his wife replied.

Nick grinned. "It must be a nasty rumor. You know I'm sweetness and light itself."

"And I must be dreaming," Jess said with a straight face.

"He can't be that bad," Sandy said.

Nick chuckled. "Be careful how you answer that, Jess, or else I *will* go for the tennis court."

"I said he's a dream to work with." Jess glanced at him. "How's that?"

"You're off the hook."

"I hope I'm off the hook with you," Sandy said to him. "About Atlantic City."

"You are."

She started laughing. "I would have loved to have been there."

"I would have loved to have had you there," Jess said sweetly.

"Now, Jess. You know I owed you."

"And now I owe you."

"I think I want a divorce," Marty said, rolling his eyes heavenward.

"On our anniversary? It isn't done, darling."

"Well, I don't want to be around when Jess decides it's pay up time. The mariachi band was the last straw."

"What mariachi band?" Nick asked.

"She gave us a mariachi band for an anniversary present last year—at one in the morning," Marty said. "If she was devising a new method of birth control, let me tell you, it works."

"Why are you complaining?" Sandy asked dryly. "You help her half the time with her jokes."

"*Once* I helped her on a joke."

"It was our wedding night, Martin Fitzgerald."

"Hold it," Nick said. This was one he couldn't pass up. He looked at Jess. "You played a practical joke on them, on their wedding night?"

"The morning after, actually," she said sheepishly. "Beyond that I plead the Fifth."

"I don't." Sandy grinned evilly. "Marty and I went to Mexico City for our honeymoon, and we had a . . . wonderful wedding night. The next morning, Marty called down for room service, breakfast for two. I thought he was so romantic. Then suddenly this voice from under the bed advises him to make it for three."

"It was a tape recorder," Jess said, giggling. "Marty very nicely turned it on at the right moment."

"It scared Sandy half to death," Marty said, the laughter bubbling up out of him.

Sandy looked so offended that Nick tried desperately not to laugh. But one look at Marty, who was already leaning weakly against the bar, and he was lost.

"I will admit that Atlantic City made up for a lot," Sandy said.

"More than you know," Nick said, and started laughing all over again.

Sandy raised her eyebrows. "Jess's description wasn't quite so interesting."

"I never saw anybody jump like that." Nick waved

his hand in a wide arc. "I thought she would go right through the wall to the next room."

"I'm surprised you didn't blast the walls out with your bellowing," Jess commented.

"I didn't bellow." She gave him a look. He shrugged. "Well, maybe a little."

"A little!" Jess gasped in clear outrage. Her eyes, though, were sparkling with mirth. "You sounded like a wounded moose."

"You hit me in my libido, Jess."

She started laughing. "Lord, but you were funny."

He grinned. "You weren't so bad yourself."

"If that was a spur-of-the-moment switch on Tony's part," she said to Sandy, "then he's got a real talent for this."

Sandy leered comically. "Among others."

Jess sighed loudly. "What a show."

"And was there ever a lot to show," Sandy agreed.

"I don't think I like where this is going," Marty said.

"I know I don't," Nick added. "I've seen the show."

"We'll be good," Jess promised, her fingers very obviously crossed.

He glared at Jess, who smiled as Sandy whispered something to her. Inwardly, he was pleased with her teasing him. Whatever had upset her earlier in the day was gone now. It occurred to him that her comment about the show could be meant to provoke jealousy. He liked the thought. Instead of being an intrusion, Sandy and Marty's presence was turning out to be very revealing. He had never realized before how much of the joy in living was found in laughter.

"It's good to see you really enjoying yourself, Jess," Marty said, echoing Nick's thoughts.

"I try."

Marty shook his head. "You haven't been like this for a long time. You always look terrific, but there's been something missing. Now, it's back."

Jess smiled.

"I have to admit that I was a little pleased about the band last year," Marty went on. "That was the first indication that you were getting back to your old self again . . ."

Her smile slowly faded.

". . . You hadn't done a joke in ages. But I can really see the old Jess aga—"

Sandy nudged her husband in the ribs, cutting him off.

"Ouch!"

"I see someone waving at me," Jess said in a rush. "I better go."

She whirled around and walked away.

"Dammit, Marty!" Sandy began

Nick didn't wait to hear the rest. He went after Jess. Right before she'd turned away, he'd seen pain in her eyes. Something in Marty's innocent compliments had upset her greatly.

He found her wandering aimlessly among the guests, nodding and smiling at anyone who happened to look her way.

She gazed blankly at him when he took her arm and said, "Let's go for a walk."

He led her to the French doors that took up an entire wall. Opening one, he drew her onto the empty lighted terrace. The night was cool and he removed his jacket and placed it around her shoulders. She stared out at the back lawn, without acknowledging his gesture.

A whimsical topiary caught his eye, and he smiled at the shrub shaped into a sitting Bambi, a butterfly atop its nose. Looking around the terrace he saw, in the soft floodlights, crocuses sprouting wildly out of the low stone wall surrounding the terrace.

"You did the landscaping, didn't you?" he asked, looking around and seeing more evidence of Jess's deft touch.

"Yes."

"I can see why Roger suggested a terrace. This one is beautiful now, but it must be spectacular during the summer with everything in bloom."

He heard her take a deep breath. "I hope you didn't bring me out here to really talk."

He stepped in front of her and gazed down at her. "I brought you out here for this."

With gentle force, he lowered his mouth to hers. He could easily sense her shock at his actions. Not wanting to give her room to think, he slid his arms under the jacket and pulled her to him. He felt her hands on his shoulders, as if to push him away. After a moment of hesitation, her nails sank into his shirt. Her lips parted slightly, and he delved into the sweetness inside.

His hands wandered down her slender back, and she moved tightly against him in response. Her breasts pressed into his chest; her long legs shifted, pulling him inside out with the sign of her inner restlessness. Her mouth greedily mated with his, and in the taking, there was a need he'd never imagined.

Suddenly, she was struggling out of his embrace. His jacket fell to the brickwork flooring. Without a word, she ran back inside the house.

"Damn!" Nick muttered, running a shaking hand through his hair. "How could I have been so stupid?"

He snatched up his jacket and strode inside. He glanced around, trying to spot her among the guests. He moved systematically through the room, but she wasn't anywhere to be seen. He even tried the bathroom, in hopes that she'd retreated there.

Nothing.

Becoming desperate, he stopped several people to ask if they'd seen her.

Finally, a blue-haired woman said, "I think I did see her in the foyer not too long ago."

"Thanks."

Scowling, Nick headed for the door.

Jess shut her front door and leaned against it in vast relief.

Poor Marty, she thought. He probably had no idea of how much his innocent remarks had sliced through her. Until he had started talking about a change in her, she had thought she'd kept her inner devils well buried. But the knowledge that she hadn't was painful to face. Even more painful was the thought of Nick hearing it all. She had had to get away.

She nearly whimpered as she remembered walking out onto the terrace with him. She'd been like a robot, trying to close herself off from everything and everyone. And then he had kissed her. She had wanted it so badly, had needed it like a drug. For a moment, she had felt safe, and then everything inside her had slammed shut—exactly as it had happened before. She had been fooling herself with all her lectures and warnings to keep away from him. She knew now that all along she had wanted Nick to be the one to rescue her from her destructive nature. Instead, she was making him pay for it.

It had been a mistake from the beginning, she admitted. And she had compounded it with the bet and going to work for him. She'd been too attracted. That had been her biggest mistake.

"What a mess," she whispered.

The only thing she could think of to do was to get out completely. Now.

Her doorbell rang.

She closed her eyes and shuddered. She knew who it was.

It rang again.

She turned around and faced the door. If she opened it, she'd be letting him into more than her house. For his sake she shouldn't.

She stared at the knob, then her hand reached out and closed around it.

Eight

Nick breathed a sigh of relief when the door finally opened. He stepped inside before Jess could invite him to do so. Maybe she would have, he thought. And maybe she wouldn't. He wasn't taking any chances, though.

"Are you all right?" he asked, frowning in concern.

She shrugged. He could easily feel the solid barrier behind the nonchalant gesture.

"I'm fine."

"Good. And you got home okay."

"Why wouldn't I?"

"You could have made a right turn to California."

"You go left for California."

"Most people don't run away after they've been kissed."

"Most people don't get kissed by their employers."

"I don't think that's the problem here, Jess," he said, staring at her.

"Of course, it's the problem," she protested, waving a hand. "I work for you. It would make things complicated and crazy to have anything but a professional relationship."

"I see. So you were upset because we have a professional relationship, and we shouldn't have a personal one."

"Right."

As she drew in an audible breath, he found his gaze focusing on her breasts.

"And that seems to be getting . . . worse," she went on. "I think the only solution is for me to give up the landscaping for MeadowHill, Nick."

That captured his wandering attention. "What!"

She lifted her chin. "I said I'm quitting. I'm sorry, Nick, but I don't think it will work anymore. The plans for the model are laid out, and Duane and Roger can finish it while you get in a new land—"

"Let me get this straight," he interrupted. "You want to give up the job because something personal interferes with our professional relationship."

"I . . . yes."

He could feel the anger building within him, and at the same time he wanted to show her just how personal a relationship they could have. He controlled both urges, knowing there was something more involved here. He was determined to find out what.

"I understand your feelings on this," he said, trying a different tactic. It was obvious she was braced for a blowup, so he would be calm and cool. Smiling, he added, "So what time should I pick you up tomorrow night?"

"Pick me up!"

"Sure. For our personal relationship."

"But we don't *have* a personal relationship!"

"Not yet," he said, grinning widely at her astonished expression. "I think you're right that our personal relationship would interfere with our professional one. But now that you've quit, we won't have that problem. Thanks for doing that, Jess. I would have hated to fire you. What time tomorrow night?"

She was motionless for a long moment, then said, "I walked into that one, didn't I?"

He nodded. "So now will you tell me the real reason you're so upset?"

"I just did."

"Bull," he said flatly. "Using our working relationship is just an excuse, and you know it. Are you seeing someone?"

"No."

"Are *you* gay?"

She actually chuckled. "No."

"Just asking." He rubbed her arm in reassurance. "Talk to me, Jess. Tell me what the problem is."

She moved away. "I can't, Nick."

"Can't? Or won't?"

"Both. It's for the best."

Despite the tears in her eyes, he willed her to explain further. She didn't.

"You'd better go now, Nick," she said quietly, not looking at him.

He wondered if it might be better to give her a little time to sort herself out. After all, it had taken him a while to sort out his own confusion about her. Still, the thought of leaving nagged at him. All along, he'd sensed an undercurrent of anxiety within her, and it was obvious that it had come to the surface tonight. Would leaving really give her a chance to come to terms with whatever was troubling her? Or would it give her time to build an insurmountable wall around herself?

"Nick, please." The desperation in her voice was clear.

He unclenched his jaw. "Okay, Jess."

She walked to the door and opened it. "Thank you for coming by. And I'll be okay now. Really."

"I expect you to be on the job Monday morning," he said, walking to the threshold.

"But—"

"No buts. We have a contract." He smiled to take any sting out of his words. "I don't want anyone else to do the houses."

She sighed. "I remember a much more hesitant man hiring me."

"Bosses are supposed to be hesitant. It keeps you employees on your toes."

"Nick, I don't think it's a good idea. For me . . . or for you."

"I'll worry about me, Jess." He touched her cheek. "You just worry about what I'll do if you're not digging up my dirt Monday."

"I'll think about it over the weekend."

"You'd better think right."

She shook her head in resignation and smiled. "Good night, Nick."

"I'm going," he muttered under his breath, trying to shake the feeling of making a mistake. Louder, he said, "Good night, Jess."

He took a step toward the cold indifferent night waiting outside her house . . . and turned around.

"The hell I'm going, Jessica Brannen."

He yanked the door from her hands and slammed it shut. Pulling her to him, he covered her lips with his in a devastating kiss.

Taken by complete surprise, Jess couldn't think to protest. All she could do was feel . . . feel the fierceness of the kiss . . . feel the overwhelming need in him . . . feel her own need rise to match it.

When the protest finally did come, it was without substance, only a weak reminder that she should not be kissing him, that her arms shouldn't be entwined about his waist, that her hands shouldn't be exploring the strong muscles of his back. Her body was flooded with yearning and pleasure, and her mind kept nudging her, reminding her of the laughter between them. She wanted him, and now she could taste the promise of satisfaction.

His hands traveled down her spine and crushed her hips to his. For long minutes, she inhaled the scent of cologne and man, tasted the tender fury of his mouth, heard the breath coming hard and fast within him. The zipper of her dress opened as if by magic, and the bodice slipped away from her aching breasts.

He buried his face in the softness of her neck, then touched her breasts with a sureness that drew the air from her body in a rush. He teased her with a string of kisses, from her hungry mouth to her tingling breasts, until his tongue was laving the hard point of her nipple. She held his head to her, driving the endless torment higher.

He finally raised his head, and she could see the need glittering in his eyes. "This is what you want between us, Jess. And more."

She wasn't sure what she wanted beyond this.

There was no denial in her, though, and she knew that for tonight she had been granted freedom from the past. She had to taste it fully before it was gone.

At her silence, his mouth came down on hers, and the intensity of their desire exploded. She was dimly aware of being lifted and carried to the sofa. Their hands shed the barrier of clothes and explored with a frenzied gentleness.

His fingers circled her nipples, tracing the sensitive points. Slowly the circle tightened until she nearly cried out from the heat he created. Then he stirred the flame higher with soft kisses. His fingers smoothed along her waist, her hips, her thighs, then his hands and mouth touched her in such ways that she became mindless with passion.

Her own hands were not idle. She delighted in the pelt of hair arrowing down his taut belly and the solid muscles of his thighs. His skin was hot, almost burning to her touch. It gave her a sense of feminine power to know she had created this fire within him.

All too soon and yet not soon enough, his hard body intertwined with the softness of hers. With each thrust, satin encased steel. As one in an ever-increasing tempo they burned brighter and brighter . . . then erupted into the searing flame of satisfaction and peace.

Jess felt warm and weightless. She sighed contentedly at nothing and everything. Slowly she opened her eyes, and the contentment instantly slipped away. She knew now what it was like to make love with Nick. She knew the intense need that only he could create within her, then placate with his passion and tenderness. But she could feel the dreaded smothering panic just beneath the surface. This time it had been crueler than before. It had stayed away just long enough for her to experience making love with Nick . . . and to damn her with the knowledge.

She began to cry. She cried for herself, for what she wanted so badly and couldn't have. But mostly she cried for Nick.

Nick felt a strange dampness on his shoulder. Dimly puzzled, he made a mighty effort and reached up to touch it. Then he heard a sob. He lifted his head to find Jess crying. Her tears shocked him out of his contented lethargy.

She was beautiful and astonishing, and she had a passion within her that had driven him beyond insanity. A voice had told him not to walk out the door, and he would be eternally grateful to that voice.

But she was weeping, and of all the reactions he might have expected after lovemaking, this one wasn't on the list.

"Jess," he whispered. He wiped away tears trickling down her cheeks. Maybe he hadn't been as gentle as he'd hoped. "I hurt you, didn't I? Lord, honey, I'm so sorry."

"You didn't hurt me," she said, wiping at her face with the back of her hand. "This never should have happened. I should have stopped it. But I was selfish, so selfish."

"I hope you'll be even more selfish in the future," he teased, hoping to find a way past her tears.

Instead, she cried even more. "No, you don't. I'm so sorry, Nick. So sorry."

He shook his head and tried to sort through her words. "I don't understand."

She sniffled back her tears. "I—I'm not normal. I can't handle a relationship with a man."

"Of course you're normal."

"No, I'm not!" she protested violently. "Look at me. Lovemaking leaves a normal person feeling wonderful and happy. All I feel is miserable."

"I can't tell you what that does for my ego," he muttered, sitting up. He reached for his trousers and pulled them on.

"I knew it," she said, gathering up her own clothes. She scooted over to the other side of the sofa and slipped on her dress. "I knew I'd hurt you somehow, and now I've done it."

He brushed the wisps of hair away from her cheek. "I'm not hurt."

She gave him a look of disbelief.

"Okay, maybe a little," he conceded. "But you're so unhappy; you have been all evening. You won't talk about it, and I can't do a damn thing to help you until you do."

"But I told you, I'm not normal. I haven't been since my divorce."

He began to piece together the tidbits she'd given so far and came to an obvious conclusion. "You mean you're afraid of being hurt again. Jess, we all have scars after a divorce. It's only natural for you to be afraid."

"This is different." She drew in a deep breath. Her eyes were wide with her vulnerability. She seemed ready to shatter all over again, and yet he sensed that whatever she had been keeping pent up inside her was about to burst out.

"I was silly enough to think that mine would be a

fairly painless shedding of an adulterous husband, who had hurt my pride more than anything else."

He smiled. "It's always more than pride and it's never painless, sweetheart. I've been there, too, remember."

She closed her eyes briefly. "He sued for an alimony that made everyone's head spin. It was bitter and messy, a landmark case in its way. And he won. The local papers had a field day during the trial, and I was prime meat for the gossip columns." She smiled sadly. "Sandy said I was dull reading, hardly enough dirt in my past to plant a marigold in."

Nick cursed at the thought of what she must have gone through.

She swallowed. "It took awhile to put it behind me. At least, I thought I had. And then a man asked me to dinner. We began seeing each other. I told myself it was only natural for him to expect something more than a good night kiss after two months of dating. It was normal for him, normal for anybody, and I knew it was time. But I . . . couldn't. He was a nice man, and yet I froze at the idea of any kind of commitment. But instead of breaking it off like a normal person would, I went out and deliberately got myself arrested."

"What!"

She nodded. "I went for a little drive on the turnpike, at a little beyond the speed limit. In the end the charges were speeding, verbally assaulting an officer, and resisting arrest. The cop and I had a disagreement about whether I was doing ninety or ninety-five. It was a little too much for my potential lover to accept, and he avoided me after that. I think I knew he would. I panicked with the next man. And the next. By the third time, I realized exactly what I was doing. The trauma of finding out my husband was cheating on me, then going through that divorce, had ruined me for any other man. The possibility of another serious relationship terrifies me so much, I unconsciously do anything I can to scare the man off. For the past year I've kept my dating to a very casual minimum. Until you."

One important fact stood out from the things she'd told him. He grinned in male pride and said, "Jess, I hate to burst your bubble, but you don't have that problem with me."

"You don't understand!" she cried. "I'm doing it now! Are you going to want to make love again, knowing I'll be miserable afterward? I won't be able to help myself, Nick. Look at what I've done so far: I've hidden in bathrooms, acted like an idiot in front of everyone because of something Marty said, run away from a couple of lousy kisses—"

"They were far from lousy, Jess."

She waved a hand. "You see? They were terrific and I insult you. I even quit my job over some stupid reason to provoke you. I won't realize what I'm doing until I really do drive you away."

Nick just smiled.

Jess awoke to bright sunlight. She uncurled from her cramped position on the empty sofa. She remembered bursting into fresh tears last night, and Nick gathering her in his arms to let her cry it out before she'd finally fallen asleep.

And now he was gone.

She climbed the stairs to the main bathroom. The

mirror revealed her blotchy complexion and red-rimmed eyes. She decided that if nothing else would have scared Nick off, her face would.

He had been so patient and kind last night, she thought. And she had been so . . . cruel. But their lovemaking had been more than physical relief of the tension between them. She had known that immediately, and had proceeded to annihilate the threads that were beginning to bind them together. If Nick's absence was any indication, she had done the job all too well.

But she didn't feel a trace of relief inside her this time. There was only pain, pain at the way he had held her when she'd started crying again, pain that she had fallen asleep in his embrace and awakened to nothing. Only now was she realizing how much he had endeared himself to her.

She knew she'd done the right thing. Nick wouldn't want to involve himself with an emotionally crippled woman. And that was the last thing she wanted for him.

She felt no better after her shower, only resigned. She put on her thick robe, took a deep breath, and went downstairs to make coffee.

She had just turned on the coffee maker when her front door opened. She watched in shock as Nick stepped inside, took a key out of the lock, and shut the door behind him. He was carrying a large bag and had a newspaper tucked under his arm.

"I thought you were going to sleep the morning away," he said. He tossed the key chain onto the table by the door, as if he'd been doing it for the last ten years.

"But . . . but . . ." she stammered, then blurted out, "You were gone!"

"Just to get breakfast." He grinned at her as he walked to the other side of the kitchen bar. He set the bag on it. "I borrowed your keys to get back into the house. Hope you didn't miss them."

"Uh . . . no, I—"

"Good." He pulled a box out of the paper bag. "I got buns and coffee. I'm not surprised you missed me, but I wanted to go to this great bakery in Langhorne. They make the best cinnamon buns and espresso—"

"But I'm making coffee," she broke in. She was still too astonished by his reappearance to think straight.

He leaned toward her. "Jess, I'm not sure we should risk our stomachs a second time."

She blushed hotly.

"Anyway, this is espresso," he went on. He took out a large container, then a small box. He set the box away from the other items. "And I got some doughnut holes for Cat."

The twinge of guilt at the mention of her imaginary cat brought her to her senses. "Nick, why are you here?"

He unfolded the newspaper and spread it out on what was left of the bar space. He began to flip through the sections, and she realized he was completely ignoring her question.

"Nick—"

"Here it is!" he exclaimed, slapping a page. "Look, Jess, it's the *Inquirer* ad with your sketch."

"My sketch?" She pulled the paper around to face her. Her original sketch of the farmhouse model, with the rose garden fronting it, took up nearly the entire half-page ad for MeadowHill. Across the bottom of the ad in bold black script was: Custom homes by Mikaris Builders. Custom landscaping by J. Brannen and Associates.

"I used the sketch copy you gave me," he said. "It looks terrific, doesn't it? They're running a full back page for the Sunday edition tomorrow."

"You didn't tell me," she muttered, staring at the ad.

"I wanted to surprise you." His hand touched her chin and lifted it until she was gazing directly into his worried eyes. "Maybe I shouldn't have. Are you angry?"

"I . . ." She smiled. "No, Nick. It's gorgeous."

"Good. Let's finish unpacking this stuff, J. Brannen. I'm starved."

She set the paper aside. "That brings me back to my question. Why are you here, Nick?"

He looked at her steadily. "Because this is where I want to be."

"Didn't all the things I told you last night sink into your brain? I cannot have a normal relationship with a man! I go to extremes to destroy it."

"And you've warned me, Jess." He took her hands in his. "I choose to ignore it. That's my problem, not yours."

"But—"

"Things have happened very fast between us, and you weren't expecting it. I'm not going to put any more pressure on you. I promise, Jess, and it's a promise I won't break. But I'm not going to disappear out of your life, either."

She knew he meant it. It was so hard to fight him,

she thought, because it was the last thing she wanted to do. She didn't hold out any hope for conquering her destructive nature, but she wished desperately that she could. At least he knew the truth about her now.

"All right," she finally said. "But whatever happens is on your head."

He grinned. "Every man should be so lucky."

Nine

"We're going to my place."

Jess glanced sharply at Nick as he drove his car. He had suggested a drive through the country, and after she had reviewed all possible implications, she'd decided that was safe enough.

He gave her a quick look, then chuckled. "Scared you with that one, didn't I? I just need to change."

She held back a sigh of relief. "I knew that."

"Right."

She didn't answer. Although she had a lot of misgivings about seeing him, she knew Nick well enough to realize that he was extremely stubborn when he wanted to be. Last night's disaster had barely shaken him, and he wasn't budging from his stand of spending time with her. She knew, too, she could trust him. He'd said he would not pressure her, and he wouldn't.

Since she couldn't convince him to stay away from

her, she could at least allow herself to enjoy his company, she thought, and settled back in the seat.

It wasn't what he'd expected.

As Nick walked with Jess down the streets of New Hope, a quaint touristy town on the bank of the Delaware River, he couldn't help glancing at her yet again in amazement. She was relaxed and smiling, stopping for a moment to look into a shop window.

Most definitely not what he'd expected, he thought.

"Nick, hold it," she said, and pointed to a hand-painted porcelain clown mask.

He waited patiently for the "ooohs" and "aaaahs" that accompanied window shopping.

She leaned closer to him and said in a low voice, "I hate those things."

He shook his head. "You hate them?"

"When I was a girl, I had a pair of them in my room. And then I saw the original *Dracula*. Every night for weeks after that, I stared at those things for hours, waiting for the blank eye-holes to suddenly glow in the dark."

"Why didn't you take them down?"

She arched her eyebrows. "I was nine, Nick, and I didn't want to be a sissy." She laughed. "Taking them down would have been admitting I was scared. Instead, I put my teddy bear outside the covers so the vampire would get him first."

"You were rotten."

"I was safe." She grabbed his arm. "I just realized this is the street with the shark shop. I have to go to the shark shop, Nick."

"Shark shop?"

"Yes, I forget the name of it exactly—something like Jaws and Junk. Wait until you see it. Everything in the shop has some kind of shark motif, including the . . . ah, powder room seat covers."

"You're kidding!"

"You'll see."

"I'm not sure I want to," he muttered.

But he was smiling as she dragged him farther along the street. After she had grudgingly given in to spending the day with him, he had expected her to be silent and distant. Even a touch of sullenness wouldn't have surprised him. When he emerged from his bedroom after changing, he discovered her curled up in his favorite chair, leafing through a builder's trade magazine. He had felt a rush of pleasure at seeing her so at home among his things. She'd seemed content, too, as they'd driven through the countryside, looking at the spring foliage. They'd wound up here in New Hope. It turned out that neither of them had been here for years, and they decided to walk through the town and explore the shops.

Sharks, he thought in amusement. There had to be something Freudian about bathroom seat covers done in sharks. He swore that if the shark on the cover had its jaws wide open for a bite, he'd buy it for her. Now that, he decided, was very Freudian.

But when they arrived, it was obvious that ON THE LAMB wasn't quite the shop Jess remembered.

"Are you sure this is it?" he asked, staring at a lamb's wool seat cover displayed in the store window.

Frowning, she glanced around. "I know it was

right next to the Hummel place. That's still here . . . . Darn it, I wanted to get a new cover for the bathroom in my father's office. He loves the one in there now, but it's falling apart."

"Somehow, little lambs in the executive bathroom don't have the same devious appeal," Nick said, grinning.

"It would ruin his image," she agreed.

"When Marty finally got around to telling me about you, he said that your father is the chairman of several boards," Nick said, casually taking her arm and steering her along the crowded sidewalk.

She nodded. "He's more of a figurehead really. Still, my divorce was very painful for him."

The only reason Nick could think of for her father to be so upset was that he had been socially embarrassed by it. He set his jaw to hold back his temper.

"You see," she went on, smiling wryly, "my exhusband was the chief executive officer for one of the companies my father's involved with, and my father introduced us. I can't convince him to stop feeling guilty."

"I don't think parents ever do," Nick said, squeezing her arm in comfort. "As the older brother, I have a lot of guilt about raising Tony. It's worse when you're a guardian. You feel you have to be perfect and make sure the kid is perfect too."

She turned and stared at him. "You raised Tony?"

"Since he was sixteen." Nick grimaced. "I thought Sandy would have told you. Our dad was killed in Vietnam when Tony was three."

"Oh, no."

"And my mother died eight years ago. Tony, naturally, came with me." He shrugged. "I wasn't ready for the teenage years."

"I don't think anybody is," she said, patting his cheek.

"I blame myself entirely for what he's doing now. I made so many mistakes. I was too strict for one thing, and now he'll do anything to show his independence, to the point of risking his future career. He thinks being with that show is the best way to put himself through law school. And I can't convince him that it will end up hurting him."

Jess made a face. "I don't see why it would. In fact, I admire him for it."

He glared at her. "You're crazy."

"No, I'm not. It's what he is inside that counts, and Tony is a very sincere and responsible person."

"And how would you know that?" Nick asked, wondering if she would confess about his brother's visit to apologize to her.

"Well . . . look at why he's doing it," she said, giving him a guileless smile. "He's determined to put himself through law school any way he can. He's not hurting anybody by stripping. It's just innocent fun for everyone, and if I'm anything to go by he makes a very good living from it."

"What do you mean, 'if I'm anything to go by'?" he demanded.

She grinned sheepishly. "I gave him a huge tip to stop him from dancing in front of me at the show."

Nick couldn't help himself. He started laughing.

Suddenly, she pointed across the street. "There's a great plant shop around the corner! I noticed you didn't have any plants in your place this morning. Maybe we ought to get some."

America's most popular, most compelling romance novels...

Here, at last...love stories that really involve you! Fresh, finely crafted novels with story lines so believable you'll feel you're actually living them! Characters you can relate to...exciting places to visit...unexpected plot twists...all in all, exciting romances that satisfy your mind and delight your heart.

Get one full-length Loveswept FREE every month!
Now you can be sure you'll never, ever miss a single
Loveswept title by enrolling in our special reader's home
delivery service. A service that will bring you all six new
Loveswept romances each month for the price of five—and
deliver them to you before they appear in the bookstores!

Examine 6 Loveswept Novels for

15 days FREE!

(SEE OTHER SIDE FOR DETAILS)

"Is this your way of changing the subject from my ne'er-do-well brother?" he asked, smiling.

"You bet. Let's go get some plants."

"I'll kill them, Jess."

"We'll get you some philodendron, then. Nobody can kill that stuff."

"Then I must have the magic touch. I've killed four so far."

"Maybe five's the trick with you," she said. "Come on."

Two minutes later, they were staring into the window of an elegant women's boutique.

"Did we get zapped into the eighth dimension or something?" Jess asked in disgust. "This was a terrific plant shop the last time I was here."

"Exactly when was the last time you were in New Hope?"

"Six years ago."

"Jessica, Jessica, Jessica," he said, shaking his head in mock despair.

"Okay, okay. I just thought the shark store and the plants would still be here. They were my favorite places."

"What other favorite places did you have in New Hope?" he asked, brushing her windblown hair behind her ear. Beautiful as her hair was, he also liked her delicate profile. "Just so I know what not to look forward to."

"Very funny, Mikaris," she retorted, stepping away from him. "Come on, I'll show you where the German bakery used to be. You'll notice I'm not taking any chances this time."

Later that evening, when Nick finally returned Jess

to her house, they were still laughing over her non-existent favorite places.

"At least the restaurant hadn't been zapped into the Twilight Zone too," Jess said as she inserted her key into the lock.

"Still, it was a close call," he said. "Your French Inn turned out to be The Squire House."

"It *was* a restaurant. Although I admit I wondered if we'd find a McDonald's there instead." She straightened and turned to him. "Thanks for the day. I really had a good time."

"So did I."

Their smiles faded, and they stared at each other.

He wanted to ignore the voice inside him, warning him that one kiss wouldn't be enough for either of them. Yet any more than a kiss would only create more pressure for her. He'd made a promise, and he had to keep it. *Still,* he thought, leaning forward . . .

He kissed her cheek.

She smiled a good-bye and slipped inside the house. He resisted the overwhelming urge to follow her and repeat last night. He knew the course of action he had taken with her would ultimately pay off. Even if it meant one hell of a lot of cold showers in the interim. Sighing, he walked back down the front steps to his car.

It hadn't been at all the kind of day he'd expected, he thought, but it hadn't been the one he truly wanted either. Except for the moment when Jess had talked about her father, she had kept the rest of the conversation neutral. He had learned a little bit more about her background. Although her parents were socially prominent, they were most fond of evenings at home . . . and their only child, Jess. He knew about her schooling, too. And last night she had told him about her divorce. But he didn't know more about the real Jess. All day long, she hadn't talked about what she was thinking or feeling, and as their time together had lengthened he'd found himself trying to steer the conversation that way. Each time she'd blocked him with a light comment before changing the subject.

He thought about her worry over doing something crazy, and he had to grin. He couldn't imagine anything she would do that would scare him away. But it was endearing to know that she was very upset at the thought. Nobody had worried about him like that for a long, long time. He liked it.

Still, she had treated him like a friend today, and a casual one at that. They had both avoided touching each other and, despite his promise, several times he'd caught himself wishing she would hurl herself into his arms and kiss him wildly. Friendship was a good place to start, he admitted, and it probably helped her to feel comfortable around him. But it also bothered him. He had a strong feeling she would keep their relationship on this level for as long as she could.

He'd let her be in control for a while, he decided.

But not too long.

"Seems to me Mikaris is hanging around the boss a lot," Roger said.

"Quite a lot," Duane agreed as he handed his coworker a fifty-pound bag of lime. "He was around her all morning."

Jess kept her mouth shut, as, on her hands and

knees, she shoved the last bag of lime to the open tailgate of the pickup truck. She hefted it over the edge . . . and let go.

"Gee, Roger," she said innocently as the bag landed on his foot. "I hope I didn't break any toes."

"Sure, Jess," he muttered, glaring at her and Duane, who was laughing.

"Now let's quit wasting time speculating on your boss's personal life and get to work," she said tartly.

"She's cracking the whip," Duane said.

"Must be serious," Roger said, and immediately jumped away from the back of the truck.

"Knock it off, guys."

Jess groaned when they didn't. It was the only drawback to the two of them, she thought. They loved to tease her. Thank goodness they didn't know about her weekend. If there had been times earlier when she'd thought she was confused about Nick, they were nothing compared to her feelings now. She was completely bewildered by herself. She should be nervous and stiff around him, yet she felt comfortable, very comfortable. When she should be closing herself off from him, she was, instead, revealing more and more. It was as if by warning him, she had now given up all responsibility for her actions. She had made love with him, and she desperately wanted to again.

And yet she was terrified of when that subconscious part of her would take over and drive him away.

"Well, well, look at that," Duane said as something behind her drew his attention.

She turned around to discover Nick helping a

woman out of a car. The woman was stylishly dressed, and Jess found herself clamping her back teeth together. Then she remembered that Nick had mentioned the interior decorator was coming today to see the model house.

"Maybe we ought to clean Jess up," Duane said. "We'd better hose her off. She's covered with lime."

"At least get the root-rot hat off her," Roger added. "Gee, how does she expect to impress a man while wearing that hat?"

"I think you two ought to have lobotomies," Jess said, glaring at them. "That happens to be the interior decorator."

The two of them merely raised their eyebrows.

Jess smiled. "Keep it up, guys, and you'll be docked a week's pay."

"You wouldn't!"

"Try me."

"Okay, okay," Duane said grudgingly. "But you look like a slob, Jess."

"Good. Maybe you two will get the hint that Nick and I have a working relationship only."

"No comment," Roger said as he pushed the wheelbarrow full of lime toward the house. Duane followed him with the large bin spreaders.

Jess sank back onto the truck bed and shook her head. Her employees were closer to the mark than she cared to think. She glanced over toward Nick and the interior decorator. *Really,* she thought as she eyed the other woman's high heels. Didn't the decorator have any sense? This was a construction site, for heaven's sake, not the Le Bec Fin restaurant.

Nick spotted her and waved. She automatically

waved back, then groaned when she realized she was still wearing her sun hat. Instant horror arose as she saw them coming toward her. She whipped off the hat and jumped down from the truck. She took several useless swipes at the white streaks of lime covering her clothes. If only she didn't look quite so disreputable . . .

Oh, forget it, she thought, and jammed the hat back on. Getting dirty was part of her job, and she'd be damned before she was ashamed of her appearance.

"This is Marilee from Custom Interiors," Nick said, introducing them.

Jess held out her hand . . . and noticed the bright red glove covering it. She yanked it off.

"I'm sorry," she said, offering her hand again.

The woman raised a perfectly arched eyebrow and gingerly touched Jess's hand for a split second. Jess wished she looked even more disreputable. Maybe that snobby eyebrow would shoot right off the woman's head.

"Mr. Mikaris tells me you're the landscaper," Marilee said. "I need to ask you about the terrace landscaping."

"Fine," Jess said, smiling politely.

"Now, how exactly will the terrace be done? In concrete or red brick?"

"Flagstone."

"But that's so . . . gray."

Jess widened her smile. "I believe that's the only color flagstone comes in."

"I'd like to suggest, Mr. Mikaris," the woman said, turning to Nick, "that you have a red brick patio with a wood overhang. We could use white wrought-iron furniture, and have pots and pots of flowers dripping down from the overhang . . ."

Nick looked over at Jess, his expression questioning. She shook her head, knowing it was all wrong for an Elizabethan farmhouse.

"I'm afraid the flagstone has already been ordered," Nick said, shrugging.

"Oh, dear. The brick patio would have made a lovely architectural statement with the old-fashioned farmhouse. I'd better look inside the house right away to see what we can salvage."

The woman shifted her briefcase meaningfully, and Nick led her away.

" 'Architectural statement' my grandmother," Jess spat, watching them go.

That woman, she decided, would ruin the house with her ridiculous "statements." Pulling her glove back on, she stalked after them.

She entered the house just in time to hear the woman say, "Let's go through the house once, very quickly, and I'll throw out my initial reactions. Then we'll go over it again more slowly and make our working decisions."

Oh, brother, Jess thought, then smiled as Marilee glanced at her.

"Now for the foyer . . ." The woman twirled around in a circle. "I see bright impressionist prints, and Louis Quatorze tables."

Jess caught Nick's eye and made a face.

Tapping her notebook with her pen, Marilee led the way into the living room. "Here, I see lovely clusters of yellow and black furniture groupings. We could do some of the fabrics in plaids."

Nick glanced over at Jess. She curled her lip in a sneer. His expression was neutral, yet she sensed he was smothering a grin.

As they moved from room to room, it became a game.

In the dining room, the decorator said, "Oriental. Definitely Oriental."

Jess rolled her eyes heavenward.

"Ultramodern," the woman said, for the kitchen.

Jess shuddered.

"The den should be heavy antiques," Marilee proclaimed.

Jess pulled her hat down over her eyes.

Girlish French provincial was the stamp of approval for the small bedroom.

Jess's hands pushed down on an imaginary dynamite blaster, then shot outward, imitating an explosion.

The middle two bedrooms were tagged as "simple contemporary."

The decorator's suggestion was tagged out.

The master bedroom "had" to be done in sleek art deco.

Jess put her hands around her throat and made a gagging motion.

Through it all, Nick's face was a study in neutrality. Jess wasn't sure with which she was having the most fun, trying to hide her opinions from the decorator, or trying to crack Nick's stony exterior.

The final touch came when the decorator suggested that the master bath be done in foil wallpaper to "surprise and delight the user's senses."

Jess crossed her forefingers and waved them around as if to ward off vampires.

Nick finally broke down. He bared his teeth at her. Jess choked on her laughter.

"Well, Mr. Mikaris," Marilee said, after they had moved into the upper hallway. "Shall we do our second tour?"

He drew in a visible breath. Jess could pretty well guess what he would say, and she smiled to herself.

"While all your suggestions have been truly . . . unique, Marilee," he said, "I'm afraid they're not what I wanted for the house."

The decorator snapped her notebook shut and folded it in her arms.

"And what did you have in mind?" she asked frostily.

"Something a little more in line with the setting, more . . ." He looked helplessly at Jess.

"What Mr. Mikaris means," Jess said, stepping closer, "is that this house, being the model, has to appeal to the buyer's senses in a particular way. It should project a relaxed, get-away-from-the-rat-race image. It's a farmhouse, and it has to have that country living charm. Laura Ashley prints for the furniture and wall coverings; baskets filled with knitting or flowers; maybe a pewter-and-wood motif in the—"

"How droll," Marilee said. "If this is what you want, Mr. Mikaris, then I'm afraid I can't help you. Custom Interiors prides itself on being in the forefront of interior design. We will bill you, of course, for our time."

"Of course," Nick said.

With a huff of indignation, the woman walked away and down the stairs to the front door.

Nick turned to Jess and advanced on her. She

smiled innocently and backed away until her bottom touched the wall.

"Now, Nick," she said in a placating voice. "You know her suggestions were all wrong."

"You got any suggestions for a new decorator?" he demanded, bracing his palms against the wall on either side of her shoulders.

"Well, no. But, Nick, she just didn't understand the house."

"Well, I have a suggestion for a decorator," he said, staring into her eyes. Their mouths were inches apart. "Since you understand the house, you can decorate it, too."

"Me!" she exclaimed.

"You. I didn't build this house as a statement, and I damn well don't want the inside ruined by some flake. You can find a decorator willing to do the gofer work, but you do the house. Have fun, Jess."

"But I'm a landscaper!"

"You've got Hulk One and Hulk Two to do the outside work. All you have to do with the house is tell the decorator what we want and make sure she gets it."

"Nick, listen—"

His kiss silenced her. Her surprise was instantly overtaken by a rush of desire. Their mouths pressed together, tasting each other in growing hunger, and Jess's mind and body were instantly filled with the sensations of their lovemaking.

When he finally lifted his head, she sighed blissfully and straightened her tilted sun hat.

"Make me a home, Jess," he said in a low voice.

"Yes," she murmured, knowing that she'd love to do it.

"Good." He kissed her lightly. "We'd both better get back to work before I forget my promise."

He walked away.

Jess sighed again and looked around the hallway. So many ideas were already running through her head. Despite the extra work, she couldn't help smiling in anticipation.

Then her smile faded slowly.

"Make me a home," he'd said.

And that, her heart admitted, was exactly what she wanted to do.

Ten

"I really can't do the decorating for the house."

Nick didn't blink at Jess's statement. He was only surprised it had taken her twenty-four hours to make it. He leaned back in his office chair and motioned to the one on the other side of the desk.

"Sit down, Jess." When she did, he added, "Of course, you will do the decorating."

"But I can't." She hopped out of the chair and began pacing the tiny trailer. "I'm really sorry about that other decorator. It was all my fault—"

"No, it wasn't," he said. "Decorating may not be my forte, but I know I didn't like what that woman had in mind for the house."

"Nick," she said impatiently, "why did you have her come in originally?"

"Because her firm was recommended to me," he said, frowning in puzzlement at her odd question.

"And if they were recommended, then it's because they're good! But I made you question her judgment—"

"You stopped me from doing something stupid—"

"I made you *do* something stupid! You had a decorator from a recommended firm come in and tell you how to show off the houses, and by clowning around, I got you to dismiss her. Now I've put you in a bind with getting the model furnished before you open it. What the hell do I know about decorating, anyway?"

"It's a sure bet I know a lot less than you," he said, grinning in amusement. "Being highly recommended doesn't mean she was right for the house."

"Don't you see? I *ruined* it for you! It was deliberately unconscious." She frowned. "Unconsciously deliberate. Whatever." She stopped and took a deep breath. "I was doing it again, Nick. I was trying to mess things up for you to get you to . . ."

"Leave you alone?" he finished for her.

She nodded.

"You're going to have to do better than that," he said, chuckling.

"This is all a joke to you, isn't it?" she asked, clenching her hands together.

"No, Jess," he said shortly. "It's very serious to me. It's so serious that I'm letting you control this relationship until you're convinced that there's nothing you can do to drive me away."

She sat silent for a long time, staring at the wall behind him. With her concentration elsewhere, he took advantage of the rare opportunity to admire the way her breasts rose and fell with each breath she took. He remembered how she had writhed beneath him in complete pleasure when they'd made love. For his own sanity, he tried not to indulge himself this way too often.

When she looked at him again, he immediately forced his features into a benign expression.

"What if I didn't have a . . . problem with men, and said to you that I felt we could only be friends?" she asked, her gaze steady on his. "Would you accept it, then, as one of those things that just wouldn't work out?"

"Would you be telling me that if you didn't have a problem?" he asked in return.

She didn't answer.

"You wouldn't." He stood up. The only thing keeping him from walking around the desk and taking her in his arms was his promise. "You know as well as I do that if that were the case, we'd be in bed right now."

She folded her arms across her breasts, pushing the enticing curves upward. His breath suddenly whistled out of his lungs at the shine of defiance in her eyes and the stubborn set of her jaw. She had a core of steel inside her that touched his own.

"I'm a challenge to you, aren't I?" she asked.

"I just know what I want, Jess." He smiled. "And I'm willing to wait for it."

"You are stubborn."

"I know. And you like it."

He walked over to her. Putting his arm around her waist, he ushered her to the trailer door.

"You did me a big favor yesterday with the decorator," he said, "even if you won't admit it. And you'll be doing me an even bigger favor if you supervise the decorating. Now get out of here, or else I won't be responsible for my actions." He tapped her hat brim. "Even that thing is beginning to look sexy."

"Wonderful," she said.

He laughed. "I wonder if anyone knows that hat has potential as an aphrodisiac."

"I think the question is how low will Mikaris go."

"As low as you like," he whispered in her ear.

"Oh, Lord," she murmured, flushing bright red.

"Trace your ancestors back to the *Mayflower* and you're left with a Puritan backlash and a pretty blush," he said. "Now we hot-blooded Greeks don't blush at anything."

"Right. I'm going back to work before I get a lecture on hedonism."

"You'd better go back to work before you get a demonstration."

"Good-bye, Nick."

He was laughing as she strode out the door.

When he finally returned to his paperwork, he just stared at it, in no mood to tackle it again. Instead, his mind wandered back to the conversation with Jess. She had asked if she was a challenge to him. Was she?

From the beginning, his attraction to her had been unbelievably strong. He had wanted her then, and if the want had been temporary, he would have been satisfied once they'd made love. He had been very satisfied, but the wanting hadn't faded. In fact, it had grown. He was suppressing it now, keeping it from his thoughts, because he had a promise to keep. For her. But the want wasn't wrapped up in a challenge, at least not a challenge to conquer a woman's sexual resistance. It was a much more tender challenge, he thought, smiling.

It was the challenge of a lifetime.

"You look terrible, Jess."

"So they tell me," she said, glaring at Sandy.

Jess hadn't bothered to stop by her home and change, but had come straight from the site to see her best friend. She'd never given a thought to her work clothes before, but everyone seemed to be picking on them lately.

Telling herself she could wonder about that later, she said, "I need your help, Sandy. I have to decorate the model."

"You!" Sandy stared at her in shock. "But I thought Nick was going to hire a decorator."

"He did." Jess grimaced as she stepped inside the house. "Never mind how I wound up being responsible. The point is, I am."

"And you want me to help," Sandy said. Her eyes were gleaming in anticipation.

Jess grinned. "I didn't think I'd have to talk you into it."

"Of course, I've seen the original plans for the house. You could really make it a showplace."

"Nick and I want it to be a home," she said swiftly, anxious to head off any notions of "forefront" decorating. Then she realized exactly how it sounded. She rushed on. "I mean, it has to look lived-in."

"You and Nick want it to be a home?" Sandy asked, smiling archly. "Well, well, well. When's the wedding?"

"I knew it," Jess muttered in disgust. "Sandy, the house has to give the illusion of relaxed and rural living. It needs a country atmosphere. And if you tease me about this or anything else to do with Nick, I swear I will move you right to the top of the list for the next practical joke."

"You're no fun," Sandy complained.

"Thank you," Jess said primly. "Now about the decorating . . ."

She explained what she wanted Sandy to do, and they discussed specific possibilities. The longer they talked, the better Jess felt. Sandy, she knew, had excellent taste. Sometimes, Jess thought, the best person for the job was an amateur.

"One question," Sandy said, while eyeing Jess's grubby sweatsuit jacket. "Do I have to dress like you?"

Jess laughed. "No, but be sensible, Sandy. It is a construction site."

Sandy nodded.

Jess's amusement subsided, and she glanced away for a moment. "I want to apologize for the other night . . . ."

"Forget it," Sandy said, smiling. "Anyway, it was Marty who opened his idiotic mouth."

"No," Jess said firmly. "It—it was me. You know why."

"Jess, when are you going to accept that you really are normal?" Sandy asked, then sighed. "Forget I said that. I'm your friend, and I understand your quirks. Heaven knows, you've been understanding of mine. But Nick is getting to you, isn't he?"

"Maybe. I don't know."

"That's good enough," Sandy said cryptically. "Stay to dinner?"

Jess shook her head. "Thank you, but no. I need a shower and clean clothes more than I need a good meal."

"It's your loss. Reva made Stroganoff."

"Save me some." Sandy's housekeeper was the best cook Jess had ever come across. It was no wonder that Sandy and Marty were always moaning about having to diet.

When she finally arrived home, Jess headed straight for the shower. Afterward, as she cooked eggs and bacon for dinner, she wistfully thought of the Stroganoff.

"This is pathetic," she said to herself, gazing at her meager meal.

The doorbell rang, and she turned off the flame under the frying pan before going to answer it.

Nick stood on her porch.

"You're not dressed for dinner yet?" he asked as he walked into the house.

"What dinner?" she asked, absently accepting the bouquet of flowers he handed her.

"Our dinner. Together. Surely, I mentioned that today." He sniffed. "Ah, we're eating in. Great!"

"Nick, you did not mention dinner," she said tartly, "and you know it."

"Well, you refused dinner last night, so I figured tonight was good. Besides, how are we going to get anywhere if you refuse to see me?"

"I didn't refuse to see you! I just spent Saturday and Sunday with you, and I need to catch up on things here."

"Good girl," he said approvingly, shutting the door. "Now we can spend every evening this week together. What's for dinner?"

She sighed. "Bacon and eggs."

"That's breakfast." He kissed her soundly on the mouth. "Making breakfast the night before has definite possibilities. Saves time in the morning for other things. I do like your style, Jess. In the meantime, since I've invited myself to dinner, I'll cook."

"Can you cook?" she asked, curious.

He put his arm around her shoulders and escorted her to the bottom of the stairs. "Yes, Virginia, there is a cook. You go up and put some clothes on. Here, I'll put those in water."

He took the flowers and left her standing there. Jess stared after him as he strolled toward the kitchen, whistling tunelessly. He shed his jacket and pushed up the sleeves of his sweater, clearly making himself at home. Protests pushed at her, yet she couldn't utter one. She admitted that she wanted him with her.

Smiling to herself, she climbed the stairs.

It took four changes of pants, five of sweaters, and three of hairstyles before she was finally satisfied with her appearance. Her outfit was not fancy, a rose-colored cashmere sweater that clung lovingly to her and a pair of soft wool pants. Still, according to her "friends," Nick saw entirely too much of Jess Brannen, Slob Landscaper Extraordinaire, so any improvement ought to be a shocker.

She came downstairs to the most delicious aroma and Nick grinning at her from the kitchen.

"I respectfully request permission to attack you," he said, eyeing her attire.

"Request denied," she said. "I'll go back up and change the sweater for a tent."

"Over my dead body. Dinner's ready."

"Really?" She glanced around and saw the dining table was beautifully set with her good china. The water glasses were even filled. "Oh, Nick."

"I like the sound of that."

"What did you make?" she asked. "Spaghetti?"

"Don't insult the cook. You were out of tomatoes, so we're having Pasta Il Pesto."

"You *can* cook!" she exclaimed in awe.

"I'm a bargain, Jess," he said, carrying a large bowl to the table. "Any way you look at it."

"Can I help?" she asked, feeling guilty that he'd fixed the entire dinner while she'd been dressing. "Make coffee maybe?"

He turned around and gazed at her solemnly. "I thought we had a conversation before about your coffee."

"One rotten cup of coffee, and the man holds it against me for life," she said loudly, taking a seat at the table.

"I have to, Jess. I only have one stomach."

"Quit jawing, Mikaris, and bring on the food."

"You have a great instinct for the social graces, Jess," he said, joining her.

"It's all in the wrist," she replied, grabbing the large pasta bowl.

She had three helpings. She couldn't resist; it was the best she'd ever eaten. Nick's pasta would give Reva's Stroganoff a run for its money, she thought.

"Next time I'll double the recipe," Nick said, after the meal was over. "A man could starve to death with you."

"I'm sorry," she lied. "It was delicious. Thank you."

"You're welcome." He tilted the empty bowl upside down. "I think. Poor Cat, there isn't a scrap left for him."

Jess swallowed. "Ah, Nick?"

He glanced up quizzically. "Yes?"

"About Cat . . ."

"What about him?"

"Well . . ." She tried to think of a way to explain her lie. The problem was she *had* lied, and she'd have to do some fast and fancy talking to make him understand why she hadn't confessed before this. Sometimes, she thought, it was better to leave things alone. "It's not important. By the way, Sandy's going to play buyer for the decorating."

"Sandy?" he repeated, shocked.

"Is there a problem?" she asked stiffly.

"No." He chuckled. "I suddenly realized that I could have asked her in the first place."

"Now you have to pay both of us as decorating consultants." Jess grinned. "I love it."

"I have the feeling you two will bankrupt me. Let's have coffee in the living room."

"I suppose we'd better clean up first."

"We'll do it later," Nick said as he stood.

Jess glanced from the pile of dirty dishes on the table to the ones she could see through the kitchen entryway. It wouldn't be a tragedy if the dishes waited for a little while.

"Okay, but I will make the coffee," she said firmly.

"It's already made."

"You're so efficient."

"I told you I'm a bargain."

A short time later, he was sitting next to her on the sofa. Their bodies were not quite touching and yet she could feel his warmth. It was a comfortable space between them, and she realized he probably knew it. She sipped her coffee. The bittersweet brew was just as good as the meal.

"I concede," she said, setting her cup down on the end table. "I'm a lousy cook."

"Yes, we know."

"Would you like hot coffee on your head?" she asked sweetly.

"Not really." Something on the news broadcast caught his attention, and he leaned forward.

Jess only listened absently to the news of falling stocks on Wall Street. Her attention was focused on Nick. She studied the clean lines of his profile and the strong column of his neck. There was a hardness, a virility to him that must have come early in adolescence. He probably hadn't lacked for dates since he was fourteen, she thought. Or sex, although she hoped that had begun later. An odd pain shot through her, and she knew instantly that it was jealousy.

She wished she could allow herself a little possessiveness with him, but she was allowing too many other things as it was. What she'd unconsciously done so far to ruin their relationship hadn't produced results, and she was grateful. She was trying so hard to watch herself, to realize when that destructiveness was taking over. But that was the problem, she admitted. She just didn't know when to stop herself, and she was terrified now of what she might be driven to do.

Nick shook his head, bringing her out of her thoughts. He sat back and turned to her.

"There's a helluva lot of stock trading going on," he said. "Makes a person wonder."

"Do you have many stocks?" she asked.

He laughed. "Everything I have is invested in MeadowHill. Real estate's a better gamble."

"Really?"

He stared at her. "You believe the stock market's better?"

"Actually, I don't know," she said, shrugging. "I'm not even sure how my trust funds work."

"For some reason, I thought you would know about money."

"I know about money," she said quietly. "I just don't know about economics. There's a difference, Nick."

"I suppose." He draped his arm around her.

She glanced at him. "Nick . . ."

"Relax." He shifted closer. "We have reached Stage Two."

"What's Stage Two?" she asked, all too aware of his thigh lightly touching hers.

"Snuggling."

"Snuggling? What's snuggling?"

"Jess, where have you been? In the Dark Ages?" He pulled her into the curve of his arm. "You put your head on my shoulder and we snuggle together and watch TV."

"You're a cheap date, Mikaris," she said, picking up her coffee cup and taking a sip of the cooled liquid.

"I was once known as a 'hot' date, Brannen."

"That's what I was afraid of," she murmured into the cup.

"I heard that." He gently pulled on her hair to get her to turn her head. When she did, he asked, "Do I detect a note of jealousy, Jess?"

"Let's snuggle," she said brightly, and laid her head on his shoulder.

"You didn't answer my question."

"I'm afraid to," she said honestly.

His strong hand covered her shoulder, and he whispered, "You don't have to be."

"I'm afraid of that, too."

"Then we'll snuggle."

He simply held her, and they watched TV. Jess could feel the strong muscles of his chest pillowing her head. The clean scent of soap and male teased her senses. She felt safe and protected.

And she felt an underlying tension.

Desire slowly swirled through her, tightening around her thighs, leadening her arms. Her breath came in deep silent sighs, causing her breasts to press against the side of his body. Her legs moved restlessly. She knew what she wanted, what she needed. She stared at her hand resting lightly on his stomach. All she had to do was . . .

Instead, they watched TV. For hours.

Finally, around eleven, he stretched his arms and yawned. "I'd better be going."

Jess lifted her head and sat up. She ignored the tremendous crick in her neck.

"It's getting late," she agreed.

He gathered up his jacket, and she walked with him to the door. He left her with a chaste kiss on the cheek. She watched him until he got into his car, and with a last wave, drove away.

She slammed the door shut.

"Dammit!" she cried. The anger she'd suppressed for the last hour finally surfaced in full force.

The whole night his hand had never once strayed from her shoulder. He'd never lifted her chin to bring her mouth to his. He'd never moved or shifted his body closer to hers.

And he'd known that it had driven her crazy.

He had kept his promise of no pressure, she acknowledged. Much as she wanted to, she couldn't blame him for turning it to his advantage. She really shouldn't be wishing he wasn't quite so honorable—or sneaky.

Jess groaned. She didn't know what to do with

him. She didn't want to hurt him, and she was afraid she would. She wanted desperately to take a chance, but knew she shouldn't. And yet his arms felt so right around her. She wanted the closeness, needed the lovemaking.

What, she wondered, was wrong with her? She'd never felt anything like this for another man. A war was going on inside her, and she just didn't understand—

Jess froze, suddenly understanding it all too well.

She was in love with him.

She slowly closed her eyes, as if in pain. It explained so much.

She was hopeful and scared. Maybe she was finally letting go of her past. Or maybe she would do something horrendous to get him away from her. She wanted to run after him and tell him she loved him, and she wanted to weep in despair.

Knowing she'd have another sleepless night of confusion, she walked into the living room. The dining room table caught her eye, and she cursed again.

On top of everything else, the son of a gun had left her with the dishes.

Eleven

"They're bronze, but they're not nearly as heavy as these two clowns are pretending they are."

Nick grinned at Jess's comment as they watched Roger and Duane struggle to set the last of the twelve large plate inlays into the freshly poured cement. When finished, the inlays, each decorated with a zodiac design, would form a circle around the base of the sundial, which was the focal point of the front garden. He knew the inlays were more unwieldy than heavy.

"They weigh a ton!" Roger gasped, as he and Duane carefully set the inlay into place, without marring the cement.

Both young men proceeded to collapse on their backs.

"I want a raise," Duane said, panting.

"A big one," Roger agreed.

"Quit moaning," Jess said, kneeling down. "You

two only have to push a spreader across a lawn and you think you need a raise."

Ignoring their protests of cruel and inhuman working conditions, she carefully wiped the cement away from the inlay with a wet rag.

"Jess, the garden will be fantastic," Nick said, smiling broadly at the beautiful centerpiece. "I think our bet was the best thing to happen to me."

"Bet?" Roger and Duane echoed, immediately sitting up.

"The Greek chorus is heard from," Jess said, leaning back on her heels. "Please, Nick, they're just young innocent boys with wild imaginations. Don't excite them about our gentlemen's agreement."

"She should ask the Mercer twins about us being innocent," Roger said, grinning.

Duane nodded. "What bet?"

Both of them turned to Nick.

"Jess and I have several agreements," Nick said. "Which one would you like to know about?"

"Nick!" Jess exclaimed, the warning clear in her voice.

Nick crossed his arms over his chest and merely raised his eyebrows at Duane and Roger.

"Ahh," said Roger.

"Just as we thought," said Duane.

Nick smiled at them.

As far as he was concerned, he too had several warnings to give, and the best way to do so was to reveal his personal interest in Jess. His own men had obviously received the message that Jess was 'Hands Off.' He'd noticed the way they kept their distance. Her employees were a little bit different.

He just wanted to make sure they understood. It seemed they did, and were pleased by it.

"I'm going in to see how Sandy's doing," Nick said. "Join me, Jess?"

She glared at him as she rose to her feet. "I wouldn't have it any other way."

When they were out of earshot, she asked, "What was that all about back there?"

"Nothing," Nick said innocently.

"My eye," she replied.

He resisted the urge to put his arm around her. While it was fine to show a personal interest in front of the men, it was not fine to have it look as if the two of them were ready to disappear for a couple of very private hours. Ground rules were essential. Men gossiped as much as women. They just didn't like to admit it.

"Nick, I'm not an idiot," Jess said. "I can take a pretty good guess at what you were doing, and I wish you wouldn't."

"Why?" he asked. "Are you ashamed?"

"That remark doesn't deserve an answer."

She stalked ahead of him. Nick swore under his breath and caught up with her just as she opened the door to the farmhouse.

"I've got some insecurities of my own," he said, smiling wryly, "and they came out with Duane and Roger."

Jess smiled back sheepishly. "Lord knows, I've got mine."

"They're not nearly as bad as you think."

"They're probably worse than I think." She glanced back out the open door. "I forgot to tell the guys something. You go on in."

He nodded, then laid his hand on her arm. "Jess, we're really making a home here."

An odd expression marred her delicate features. "I know."

She walked away, leaving him bewildered. And it wasn't the first time, he thought. She'd had these odd moments, ever since he'd made dinner for them last week. She wasn't cold or withdrawn. He couldn't quite define what the mood was; he was only aware of a subtle change in her every so often. That was the problem with being a man, he thought. Men didn't understand subtlety.

He'd managed to keep his promise that night, and all the nights after. Somehow. It was all he could do sometimes *not* to touch her. He didn't dare think about it in her presence. When this was over, he was going to demand a medal. He certainly deserved one.

Still, something was happening with her, and he wished he knew what it was.

"What do you think of the foyer?"

Nick glanced up to find Sandy walking toward him, her hands outstretched. He looked around and instantly spotted the pictures hanging from the walls.

He walked slowly along the plastic-covered floor, smiling more broadly with each picture. Interspersed with formal portraits were whimsical pastorals, all somehow blending together to give a feel of real people actually living in the house.

"Sandy, you're a genius," he said.

"Not me. Jess picked them. I'm the gofer, remember."

Although he had known Jess would do a terrific

job decorating, he hadn't known exactly what the final result would be. Now, seeing the interior begin to take shape, he couldn't help grinning like a little kid.

"You look very pleased," Sandy said with satisfaction.

"I am. Extremely."

"Good. I'm entitled to pump then. What's going on with you and Jess?" she asked point-blank. "I can't get a straight answer out of her."

Nick stared at Sandy for a long moment. He'd thought Jess would have confided something to her best friend.

"I don't like it," he answered finally.

"Like what?"

"That she's not telling you anything."

Sandy smiled. "Then there's something to tell."

"Maybe," he said. "Has she seemed . . . moody to you?"

"Not moody." Sandy's brows drew together as she mulled over the question. "More off in space. Why?"

"Never mind," Nick said, hearing the latch on the front door click open.

As Jess entered the foyer, Nick gazed at her in pleasure. It was amazing what cement-streaked jeans and a sweatshirt could do to the libido, he thought. Especially when they encased Jess's body. Maybe it was the way the loose sweatshirt hinted at the curves of her full breasts. Her jeans fit her enticing thighs perfectly. His hands had traveled their satiny length until . . .

"So what do you think?" Jess asked.

"Beautiful," he said absently, staring at where the

jeans met at the top of her thighs. The room suddenly seemed twenty degrees hotter.

Jess smiled at him. He smiled back.

"Shall I leave?" Sandy asked.

Nick drew in a deep breath, knowing the minute of pleasure he'd allowed himself was over.

"Stay," he said, admitting silently that Sandy's presence wouldn't make a difference. He was held by his promise. For a little longer. "I never did ask you, but how's Marty?"

"Yes," Jess said. Her cheeks were as warm as he felt. "How is Marty?"

"How's Marty!" Sandy exclaimed, throwing her hands up. "You two tease and taunt me with whatever's going on between you, and then you have the nerve to ask how Marty is?"

"Right," Nick agreed, chuckling at Sandy's indignation. "How's Marty?"

"I give up. Marty is fine, considering that he's going crazy at the moment."

"Why?" Jess asked. "What's wrong?"

"The stock market. Haven't you heard?"

Nick shook his head as Jess said, "No."

"Stocks are dropping like a dive-bombing jet. Marty called me to cancel our lunch date. His clients are in a panic."

"But it's made wild day-to-day swings before," Jess said.

"Not like this, Marty says." Sandy grinned. "Good thing you and I have blue-chip trust funds."

Jess nodded.

Nick said nothing.

"Now that I've been the only forthright person in

the room, can we go in and decide on the living room motif?"

Nick didn't join them as they began to walk into the other room. Jess turned around, a puzzled expression on her face.

"Nick?"

"I have to make a call," he said, and headed for the office trailer.

Sandy's comment "Not like this" had caught his complete attention. While he had very little in stocks, he knew his MeadowHill investors did.

A short while later, he hung up the phone. Marty had sounded frazzled, but he told him nobody could figure out why it was happening. It seemed to be only panic selling, and the experts Marty had spoken with were positive the situation was temporary and the effects would be marginal.

So far.

Jess set her napkin on the table and said, "Nick, I know I cooked it, but it can't be that bad."

He stopped pushing his broccoli around his plate and smiled at her. "Dinner is delicious. My stomach's in shock."

She chuckled dryly. "And if I believe that one, then you've got a bridge to sell me, right?"

He grinned.

"Something's been bothering you all day," she said. "What's wrong?"

He set his fork down. "Nothing. Just a little tired. I've been pushing it lately."

"Grant's Tomb must be up for sale too." She

couldn't stop the sarcasm from creeping into her voice.

Nick raised his brows. "Jess, I just said I'm tired tonight. I *am* tired, okay? Think of it as great leftovers for Cat."

"Right." She rose and picked up her plate. "If you're tired, then dinner's over. Time to go."

"I may be tired, but you are obviously cranky."

"Cranky is for three-year-olds, Nick. I'm angry."

"Angry! What for?"

"Nothing, okay?" She grabbed his plate with her free hand and headed for the kitchen.

He came after her and snatched his plate back. Picking up the fork, he began to eat and talk at the same time. "I'm eating, Jess. See? I just needed something to spur my appetite."

"That still doesn't explain what you're brooding about."

He sighed. "Jess, *you've* been brooding all week."

"I—" She stopped herself, knowing her protest would be as false as his had been. She had been brooding and tense and more than ready for an argument. Even if she had to start it herself.

"You show me yours, and I'll show you mine," he suggested.

She smiled reluctantly and shook her head. She wasn't ready to tell Nick she was in love with him. She was having a hard enough time accepting it herself.

"Okay," he said. "We keep our secrets until we're ready to talk about them."

He looked a little too relieved, but she had no right to object.

"Finish your dinner, and I'll clean up," she said.

"I'll clean up later."

She laughed. "Nick, that's the best line since 'The check is in the mail.' Bring in your plate when you're done."

She left him staring in astonishment. In the kitchen, though, her amusement faded. Nick was right, she thought as she readied the dishes for the dishwasher. She was cranky. And she knew why. One moment he would look at her with hunger in his eyes, and the next it would shut off, replaced by only friendly interest. She had nearly flung herself into his arms when it had happened today in the model house.

She glanced across the counter into the other room. Nick was clearing off the rest of the table. She watched as the muscles of his back stretched and knotted under his khaki shirt. It was always like this, she thought. She only had to look at him, and desire would swirl thickly through her body. The temptation to touch him would be irresistible.

And she would do nothing.

It was her own fault, she admitted. She had asked for control of their relationship, and she'd received it. Most women would be thrilled. Most women didn't have her problem, though. She was beginning to wonder if she needed a real burst of machismo from him to get her over it. A little seduction to absolve her of responsibility for her actions. It was silly, she thought, but his promise was making her crazy.

During her sleepless nights, she had the overwhelming urge to trust in her hope. She was so happy . . . and so confused. She'd never expected to fall in love, and she wasn't sure what to do. Or what she *would* do. The idea of it occupied her mind continually, as she tried to second-guess herself before anything disastrous happened. Probably the worst manifestation of her problem had been her crying jag after their lovemaking. But she was terrified she'd cry again, and that was holding her back.

Nick walked into the kitchen and set the dishes down on the counter.

"A clean plate," he said. "Are you happy?"

She grinned. "Ecstatic. There's hope for me yet."

He chuckled, then glanced into the other room. "Since you insist on cleaning up, mind if I catch the news?"

"No." Her grin broadened. "Go be a chauvinist and leave the little woman with the dishes."

"Witty, Jess."

"You'll catch on to it eventually, poor thing."

He left the kitchen, and after cleaning up, she joined him. She deliberately snuggled next to him on the sofa. He looked at her in surprise before putting his arm around her.

"We could easily turn into old fogies," he said, amusement rumbling in his chest.

"A little peace and quiet never hurt anybody."

She began to trail her forefinger across the width of his chest. Her finger lingered, as if tempted, on a closed button of his shirt.

"Why do I have the feeling there's a lot the old fogies aren't telling?" Nick asked the room. "What are you doing, Jess?"

"Snuggling," she murmured. "I think I've got the hang of it."

"I know you have."

He set her hand aside. Slowly it drifted back to toy with his button again.

He picked up her hand and placed it firmly on her thigh. Her hand crept back, this time lower, at his belt.

"That's it!" he exclaimed, holding her wayward hand down on her thigh with his own.

"What?" she asked innocently. She couldn't quite keep the laughter from her voice.

"You know what. Behave yourself."

"You mean my hand? But, Nick, I was just resting it on your stomach."

"Well, now you can rest it on your thigh."

She yanked her hand out from under his. Unprepared for her sudden maneuver, he snatched at her hand. Laughing, she ducked and dodged her hand through the air, managing to get little touches in as she kept it out of his reach.

She got one little touch too many, and he finally grabbed her, his strong fingers tight around hers.

"Ouch!"

"Now will you behave?"

Her mirth subsided, and she gazed into his dark eyes. In the silence, she watched desire glitter in them.

"No."

His mouth was only inches away, and she closed the space between them, brushing her mouth lightly against his.

A bare taste, then another.

She applied more pressure.

Her tongue feathered across his bottom lip.

Nick shuddered violently and pulled her into a tight embrace. His mouth moved hungrily against hers. Their tongues mated urgently in fierce, rising need. Her hands swept up and around his neck, clutching with the force of the storm running through her. Faintly, through the rushing in her ears, she could hear the television playing to an uncaring audience. The scent of him beleaguered her senses, the taste of him filled her with hunger for more.

She didn't care that she was testing his limits. She wanted to, needed to. She had to know he wanted her as badly as she wanted him. And if he broke his promise—

Suddenly and unbelievably, he pushed her away. He did it very gently, but the pain couldn't have been greater if he'd slapped her.

In the tense silence, they both gasped for breath. He rose from the sofa and she watched numbly as he got his jacket.

He turned around. "I made a promise, and I won't break it."

"What if I want you to?" she asked.

"That's a hypothetical question. I love you. You know where to find me when you're ready to ask that question for real."

The door closed behind him.

Nick sat in his darkened living room, grinning.

It was very obvious Jess had tried to get him to break his promise. Of course, she'd never admit it. She would probably be shocked at the notion. She'd be even more shocked at how close she had come to achieving her goal.

His satisfaction subsided, and he frowned. Frustration at too many nights of chaste kisses and embraces had nearly erupted tonight—with very little encouragement from Jess. But encouragement was all she'd given. It wasn't enough.

She had to come to him, not in seduction, but of her own volition. It was the only way he could see for her to overcome her fears. He hoped he was right.

He wondered if he should have stayed and talked with her instead of walking out. The last thing he had needed, though, was for her to continue her teasing.

It was impossible to guess her reaction to tonight, and he didn't even try. Still, he couldn't help wishing he knew what it would be.

His doorbell rang.

He stared at the door, then shot out of his chair. He skidded to a halt in front of the door and yanked it open.

Jess stood on his porch. Despite the mild night and her heavy jacket, he could hear her teeth chattering.

He breathed her name and guided her across the threshold and into his embrace. He closed the door, shutting out the world.

"You're here," he said in awe. Of all her reactions, this was the one he hadn't dared to consider.

"I'm scared," she whispered. "I love you, and I'm ready, and I'm scared to death."

"Just remember there's nothing you can do to chase me away, Jess."

She raised her head, her brown eyes wide with her emotions. "I hope so." She swallowed. "I'm asking for real, Nick."

He grinned. "I know."

She started to laugh, thin and reedy at first, then stronger. He joined her.

"You stinker," she said, her laughter finally subsiding into smiles. "You knew I was going to come here."

"Prayed would be more like it," he said, glad that he had made her laugh. It had dispelled the worst of her fear, and he wanted to keep it that way. "What the hell took you so long?"

"I couldn't find my car keys."

"That eager, eh?" He drew her into the living room.

"Well, you looked so desperate I took pity on you."

"Thank you."

"You're welcome."

When they reached the living room, he took off her jacket and tossed it on the chair.

Slowly, she reached up and touched his cheek.

"I love you, Jess," he said, his voice already husky with need. "I know what it took for you to come here tonight, and I'm proud of you."

"It was the hardest thing I've ever done in my life," she admitted.

"I'll make sure it's the best thing you've ever done in your life."

"Another promise?"

"I'm very good at keeping them."

She smiled. "I know."

He took her hand and together they walked into his bedroom. He knew he could easily carry her in his arms. There would be great pleasure in that, but there was more pleasure in knowing that she was walking with him, next to him, that she no longer required the promise.

They faced each other beside the wide bed. His bed. He searched her face in the darkness, unable to see yet sensing a need the same as his own. He lowered his head.

His lips touched hers softly, gently. She had said she was scared, and he could sense the effort she was making to keep her fear under the surface. He teased her with little kisses at first, allowing her time to trust in the instinct that had brought her to him.

His mind, however, reeled with satisfaction at her presence. And her words. She loved him. Weeks ago he'd questioned her abilities out of his own hurt pride, then later he'd ignored her wishes that she be left alone. He had acted with total machismo, and he vowed to spend a lifetime making up for it.

Her arms crept around his shoulders, her hands touching his back in a tentative caress. He slanted his mouth across hers, searing the promise of restraint to final ashes. His tongue darted and danced with hers. She melted against him, her body soft and yielding.

He broke the kiss and drew in a deep breath, loving the feel of her full breasts pressing into his chest, her slender thighs brushing his. His body was mindlessly pushing at his control. He forced himself to ignore it. He would not rush this night.

Slowly, with infinite care, he unbuttoned her blouse, allowing himself the heady enjoyment of revealing her satiny flesh. Lower and lower he went, to the valley between her breasts, to the silk of her waist. The back of his hand lightly touched every inch of flesh as he slid each button through its hole. When he finished the last, he pushed the blouse away.

Her skin gleamed like warm alabaster in the faint darkness. His hand leisurely coursed its way upward, around the slender indentation of her waist, the narrow column of her ribs, the delicate thrust of her breast, the sweet puckering of her nipple. She moaned and buried her face in his chest.

"Jess." His voice was hoarse with want as he ran his thumb around the ever-tightening point. He cupped her breast, adoring the way it nestled in his hand.

"You feel so right, Nick," she whispered. "Nobody ever felt right before."

It was too much. He covered her mouth with his in a voracious kiss. It was sweet and rich, lingering and exciting. He couldn't get enough of her, he thought dimly. He never would. He pulled her to him, his fingers spreading across her back. He could hear the tiny noises of pleasure she made in the back of her throat, could feel the hunger of her mouth. Perfume and woman swirled through his senses. He wanted all of her warm and soft and naked against his own flesh now, and he turned her onto the bed.

Her hands were gentle and assured as she unbuttoned his shirt and pushed it from his shoulders. His fumbled with her jeans. He tried to concentrate . . . and immediately lost himself to her touch as she stroked his bared chest. He had to push her hands away, so he could finish his task.

When they were freed of the last barrier of their

clothes, Nick heard a moan of excitement from her that matched his own. Her flesh burned his everywhere they touched. The taste of her was incredible, unique, and he neglected nothing. His hands and mouth found her breasts, belly, the curve of her hips, the slim thighs . . . the mound of her femininity. He lingered with each kiss, wanting to imprint all of her in his brain forever.

Her smooth legs entwined with his hair-roughened ones. Her lips left a string of tender biting kisses on his neck, shoulders, and chest. Her hands caressed him to a white heat.

He felt no anxiety in her, no fear. She was giving of her passion, and taking joy in his.

He covered her body with his and sank into her warm moist depths. He had wanted to absorb her into his love, and now she was absorbing him into hers. His blood roared clamorously in his ears as her body stroked him lovingly with each movement. She danced with him in the ageless ritual, and they drove each other higher and closer until they convulsed together.

As he gladly gave over his heart and body into her keeping, he knew there was no safer place for them than with Jess.

This time she laughed.

"Why," he asked, "are you laughing?"

"I can't help it," she said, the giggles escaping her. "I was just remembering our first meeting."

"As long as you're not laughing over my performance," he grumbled good-naturedly, kissing her neck.

"Never." She sighed languorously. "If you had done this in the hotel room . . ."

"When I saw you in that flimsy slip, I nearly did."

"You were so outraged."

He started laughing. "And you were so bewildered."

"And Tony was having the time of his life."

"Kid brothers are rotten." He raised himself on his elbows and gazed down at her. "How do you feel?"

"In love," she said, gazing back.

"Scared?"

"A little." She was silent for a moment. "I'm trusting my heart, Nick."

"I wouldn't have it any other way."

Twelve

She wondered if everyone knew.

Probably, she thought, smiling to herself. If they didn't know by the silly expression that must be on her face, then they knew by Nick's. Even from here in the garden, she could see his wide grin as he talked with Sam by the office trailer.

"Jess, at the rate you're going, we won't have the bushes planted until *next* year," Duane said, setting rosebushes two feet apart in the long trench dug earlier.

"Sorry." She held a bush upright, and Roger, the third person in the assembly line, slapped the soft earth around the base of the bush.

"Leave her alone," Roger said. "Can't you see she's in love?"

Jess stared at him. Everyone might know, but she wasn't sure she wanted them to talk about it.

"Hell, I'm in love, and I'm not allowed to slack off," Duane grumbled.

"Are you really?" Jess asked, transferring her stare to him.

"Why do you think he's rushing us through this?" Roger asked. "He wants to get off early so he can see his sweetie."

"Roger couldn't get a 'sweetie' if he paid her."

"I, my friend, am playing the field. And it's a big field." Roger gave a loud sigh of contentment. "A rose by any other name looks the same in the dark. Which you will discover in about another week, pal."

Jess smothered a grin as her employees continued to taunt each other. She glanced over at Nick again. Her "rose" was unique, night or day, and she knew it. They had been together for a week now, and she was learning more and more to trust in her heart. She still had moments of panic that she was lulling herself into a false sense of security. But Nick was so steadfast and so confident in her that her panic was fading. She was really starting to believe that she might have found a cure. Maybe she'd been right before and her crying had been the worst. Was it love that had made it so different?

She thought so. She hoped so.

"Jess, Mikaris wants you."

She looked up to see Nick motioning to her. She rose to her feet and brushed off her hands.

"Don't be too long, Jess," the guys singsonged in falsetto.

She ignored their knowing smirks and walked across the road.

"I've got some bad news," Nick said, smiling at her. His eyes seemed to devour her. "The cement mixer is shot, so we can't pour the terrace today."

"Fine."

She was mesmerized by the way little wisps of his chest hair curled around the collar of his T-shirt. Funny that she'd never noticed before. She should have. It was sexy, and she had the urge to reach out and . . .

"We'll have to get a new one," Nick said in a husky voice. "What the hell."

"We'll be another day late!" Sam exclaimed, waving his arms in the air. They both turned to stare at him. "Somebody lifts half the two-by-fours over the weekend, Randy backs the forklift over the other half, and the cement mixer goes. And you say 'What the hell'! Geez, will you two just get married and start fighting like everyone else? Then maybe we can get some work done around here!"

Complaining under his breath, he stomped away.

"He's had a bad day," Nick said.

"It certainly seems like it," Jess agreed.

He gazed at her. "I never realized how thick your lashes were before."

She could feel her cheeks heating. "Thank you."

He sighed. "I wish we weren't so damn responsible. Otherwise I'd suggest we go home and get into a nice warm bed."

"Sam doesn't seem to think we're responsible. By the way, I'll have to force the roses to bloom."

"Is that good?"

"No. It could kill them."

"You can always plant new ones."

"That's what I figured. Everyone knows, you know."

"Knows what?"

"That we're together."

"I don't see how they could miss it. I've been walking around with a sappy grin on my face." He grinned sappily. "Do you mind?"

She shook her head. How could she? She felt like a schoolgirl with her first crush—only better. It was silly, but she couldn't help it.

"I want so much to touch you," he said, "but I can't. Come in to the office with me."

"That's asking for trouble and you know it." They avoided the office assiduously.

"Just for a minute."

"It would never be a minute."

"Okay, then an hour."

She shook her head. "I'd better go kill some roses before this conversation gets out of hand."

"Not out of hand, Jess. *In* the hand!"

"I'm going."

Laughing, she walked back across the road.

"She's back. She's smiling. She's rosy-cheeked," Roger said, as she approached them. "Must have been one heck of a conversation."

She took her place and held the rosebush for him. "The cement mixer's broken. They can't pour the terrace until they get a new one."

"Gee, Jess, if you looked any more unhappy, you'd float away. Ah, sweet love be thine companion always."

"Cut it out and get back to work," she ordered sternly.

"Well, I'm glad about the mixer," Duane said. "Maybe we can knock off early."

She was hoping for the same thing herself.

"But we need to go look at bedroom furniture!"

It was just after the lunch break, and Jess had gone through the house with Sandy to check its progress. Now, they were standing by the open front door. Duane and Roger were almost ready to plant more roses, and she needed to get back with them. Sandy, having made her pronouncement, was glaring at her.

"Not tonight, please." Jess was desperate. "Sandy, tomorrow. I promise."

Sandy eyed her suspiciously. "You've been promising for a week now."

"I know." Jess sighed heavily, knowing she'd put off the chore for as long as possible. "Tomorrow. I'll get off my deathbed if I have to."

"That's not the bed you'll have to get out of, and you know it."

"Sandy!"

"Sandy!" Sandy mimicked wickedly. She was grinning. "You're happy."

Jess smiled. "Yes."

"I love it. But I have enough sense to know you'll probably have one heck of an excuse for tomorrow."

"No, honestly—"

Sandy held up a hand. "I'll make it easy for you. You and Nick go out and look at bedroom furniture."

"Nick!"

"Yes. Actually it's a great idea." Sandy reached over her shoulder and patted herself on the back. "Wonderful thought, old girl."

"Sandy, I don't know . . ."

"Think of it as an adventure, Jess."

"It sounds more . . . domestic to me," Jess pointed out.

"Couldn't hurt."

Jess wondered if she was surrounded by pushy matchmakers. First Sam, and now Sandy. It was enough that she was beginning to trust her heart. She wasn't asking for more. And she didn't know if Nick was, either. They'd both tried marriage, and it hadn't worked. For all she knew, Nick had vowed never to marry again. As for herself . . . She was startled to discover it was easy to imagine being Nick's wife.

Sandy's voice rescued her from her disconcerting musings.

"Oh, go ahead, Jess. The two of you will have fun, and you can justify it by saying that it's for the model, not for yourselves."

That was true, she thought.

"Well . . ."

Her voice trailed away as she spotted through the open doorway a gleaming black Lincoln Town Car pulling into the site.

"Must be more prospective buyers," she said. "We've had several since the ad ran."

"I know," Sandy said. "And the model isn't even open yet. Isn't it great?"

"Great," Jess said, enthusiasm draining from her as two men emerged from the vehicle.

Even from the distance, she could discern one was young, the other older. Something in the stance of both, though, gave her a cold shiver. She somehow sensed that they weren't house-buyers. They never looked once at the finished model or the house in progress. Instead, they were deep in conversation as Nick strode over to them.

Nick's worried frown as he greeted the younger man only confirmed her apprehension. She watched as he was introduced to the older man, then the three of them disappeared into the office trailer.

"I wonder if they're a gay couple," Sandy said.

"I would love it if they were," Jess said, praying silently.

Twenty minutes later she was on her rosebush assembly line again when she saw the two men emerge from the trailer. Both of them looked grim. Nick didn't come out.

Something was definitely wrong.

"Guys, I need to see Nick about something," she said, dropping the rosebush into the trench and standing up.

"But we're almost done, Jess!" they both yelled.

She barely heard them as she began to walk across to the office. The trailer door was suddenly flung open, and Nick bellowed for Sam. Jess hesitated. Sam trotted over, listened for about three seconds to whatever Nick was saying, then erupted into a volley of shouting and arm-waving. He was talking so fast that the words mostly blurred together—except for two.

"Close down? Close down?"

Jess was rooted to the spot. Close down? Close down what?

"Not the site!" she breathed, and began running.

Nick turned away from Sam in midargument and headed for the truck. Jess veered in his direction.

"Nick!" she shouted.

She knew he must have heard her, but he never looked around. Instead, he got into the truck. She ran up behind it, waving her arms and shouting for him to wait. He didn't. The truck roared to life and sped away, leaving her literally eating dust.

"Jess!" Sam exclaimed as he ran over to her. "You okay?"

"He didn't wait," she mumbled, shocked at Nick's rudeness. She stared after the truck. "He didn't wait."

"I don't think he heard you." Sam smiled gently at her. "I don't think he hears anything right now."

"What happened, Sam? Who were those men? Close down what? The site?"

Sam nodded. "That was Tommy Sayers and his banker. Tommy's one of Nick's backers for Meadow-Hill. Was, I guess, is better. Tommy just pulled out."

Jess stared at the foreman. "But why?"

"All Nick would say is that the man has his own problems. Nick told me to close down the site and put the men on standby."

"For one backer pulling out?" It was incredible, Jess thought.

Sam nodded again. "Nick's either got to get the other backers to put in more, or find a new one real quick. In the meantime, we shut down. The labor costs kill the cash flow."

Jess closed her eyes. *Poor Nick*, she thought. Everything had been going so well for him, and now this. It was a disaster. She took no consolation that it wasn't something she had caused. Nick was in trouble.

"Did he go to talk to his other investors, do you know?" she asked, opening her eyes and looking at Sam.

"I don't know. Probably he just needed to get away by himself and think. I'd better go tell the men we're shut down, and then I've got to go home and tell my wife. We just bought new living room furniture." He grimaced. "Looks like we'll be eating soup for a while."

Jess swallowed back her horror. She had been thinking only of Nick, but this would affect everyone.

She straightened her backbone. "Nick will have us back working in no time. Now I'd better get the roses in and burlapped."

Sam whipped around. "But we're shut down."

"The construction is shut down. I make the decisions on the landscaping," she reminded him. Smiling, she added, "Besides, if we don't get the roses in now, we'll have another disaster when Nick reopens."

Sam chuckled.

As Jess walked away, she decided Roger and Duane would have to finish the roses without her.

She was going to Nick's.

Nick pulled into a driveway and was briefly surprised to find it was the one attached to his house. He didn't know where he had been or how he'd managed to find his way home. The numbness that had begun the moment he had spotted Tommy hadn't abated. It was worse.

He became aware of someone hurrying around the front of his truck, silhouetted by its lights, then realized it was Jess. It was dark and had been for some time. He glanced at the truck clock. It was after midnight.

Jess banged on the window. "Nick, where the hell have you been? Are you okay?"

Slowly, he opened the door and climbed out of the cab.

"Where were you?" Jess asked, as she pushed past him to reach into the truck's interior. The truck lights snapped off. "Nick, where were you all this time?"

"Maryland, I think." He began moving toward the house.

"Maryland! What were you doing in Maryland?"

"Running out of gas." He rubbed his forehead, suddenly aware of a tremendous headache.

"Are you all right?"

"Yes. No." He turned around and pulled her into his arms. He had to hold her. "Think you could love a man who's a millionaire and broke at the same time?"

"Yes." She burrowed against him, her arms wrapping tightly around his waist. He could feel the warmth of her seeping in and curling through his frozen veins. Not ready to talk, he held her for long minutes in the dark silence.

"I could hold you forever," he whispered into her hair.

"Could you hold me forever in the house?" she asked, her voice muffled against his shoulder. "My feet are freezing."

He laughed. And as he did, the strength seemed to flow back into his body. He had been helpless, as if the earth had fallen away from his feet without warning. Now just knowing that Jess loved him was like a lifeline pulling him back to safety.

After they were inside the house, Jess asked, "Have you eaten?"

He shook his head.

"Well, the world's worst cook will whip up a midnight snack."

"All I need is a bottle of whiskey and some aspirin."

"The aspirin you'll get, the whiskey you won't."

She headed for the kitchen before he could change his order to straight whiskey.

He shed his jacket and followed her. "Jess, I'm not hungry."

"You need to eat. You deserve a little pampering." She flipped on the kitchen lights and pulled open several cabinet doors before she found the canned soup. She grabbed one and turned around. "Sam told me one of the backers pulled out."

"Tommy Sayers."

"The jerk," she said succinctly.

"Tommy's a stockbroker and a heavy player in the stock market. He got creamed last week when the market took that tremendous plunge. He lost almost everything."

Jess sucked in her breath. "The idiot."

"He had to pull out. So much for Marty's experts saying the effects would be marginal." Nick was silent for a moment. "He called in the loan."

Jess stared at him, wide-eyed. "But he can't do that!"

"Yes, he can." The emotions he'd kept bottled up inside him during the hours of driving finally burst through. "The bastard says, 'Gee, Nick, I'm really sorry I blew everything.' He's calling in the loan for the money he's already invested."

He uttered a string of obscenities that left him feeling better and more angry at the same time.

Jess wisely didn't comment on the language. She set the can down on the stove and walked over to the sink. After filling a glass with water, she took down the aspirin bottle from the window ledge and shook out two. She handed the glass and pills to him and said, "But you have a contract or something that says you have so many days to pay him back, right?"

"Thirty days. Unless I find somebody to replace Tommy before the end of the week, I'll have to close out the business account to pay him. He needs the money now."

"But how can he do that to you?" Jess exclaimed.

"If he doesn't get out immediately, his creditors could claim the entire project as part of his assets. Actually, he's doing me a favor by getting out completely."

He sat down heavily on a kitchen chair and swallowed the aspirin. The whiskey would have put him out of his misery much faster, he thought. When he spoke again, his voice was flat.

"I've seen places where there's a ten-foot stretch of paved street with a model house, the windows busted out of it and piles of dirt all around it, overgrown with weeds. You've probably seen them, too."

She nodded.

Lifting his head to look at her, he went on. "You know the builder went belly-up. It's common enough, especially since there's a big housing boom going on. Some guys get greedy, and they think it's a sure thing. Every time I see an abandoned site, I vow it will never happen to me. I'll make sure my backers are solid and my homes saleable. But now it's my turn to go belly-up."

"You'll get another backer, Nick," she assured him.

"If I'm extremely lucky, and even then I doubt it'd be in time. Everybody's going to hang onto their money after last week's fiasco. And if anything else happens, they'll want to get at their money fast, not have it tied up in a long-term investment like housing construction.

"I've got men to pay and no cash." He laughed bitterly. "Hell, and I really am supposed to be a millionaire. I've never seen the money, but they tell me it's right there in the property, the trucks, the backhoes, the cranes, the bricks, the siding. The truth is, I've got enough personal cash to pay my men for about a week, two at most. If I shut down too long, they'll get other jobs, and I'll be without a crew."

"I'll be the new backer," Jess said, in a matter-of-fact voice.

Nick snapped his head up. She was facing the stove and stirring the soup. He didn't even have to think about his answer.

"No."

She turned around. "Nick, come on. You need a backer. I want to be the backer."

"No, Jess."

"Why?" she demanded, dropping the spoon into the pot.

"I won't take your money, that's why."

"Because I'm a woman?"

"Because I love you. I don't want your money, Jess. I want you."

"Come on, Nick. I have a stake in MeadowHill, too! I wanted the landscaping job from the beginning because it would help my reputation as a landscaper. I need that backer as much as you do. And I know it's a damn good investment, so why can't it be me who's the investor?"

"Jess, please." He curled his hands into tight fists. It would be so easy to say yes. He needed a replacement backer. This minute wouldn't be soon enough. But not Jess. His pride wouldn't allow him to do it. He'd never needed help before, and he seriously doubted if he would be able to live with himself if he took this kind of help from her. "I appreciate the offer, and it's tempting . . . ."

"But?" she prompted, clearly angry.

"You wouldn't really be a backer, would you? You'd just be helping me. I need to have some pride, Jess. I wouldn't have it if I took your money."

"Get it through your head that you are not taking money from me! I would be making an excellent investment. Unless, of course, you think MeadowHill *isn't* an excellent investment?"

"Of course it is!" He rose from the chair and began to pace the kitchen. "I don't want to fight with you, but dammit, I would be taking your money no matter how I look at it! No help, Jess, and that's final."

She glared at him. He walked over to her and smiled crookedly, then took her in his arms. She was stiff and unyielding.

"I was ready to quit until you started arguing with me," he said gently. "Thanks, Jess."

She sighed and put her arms around him.

"I'll find another backer, you'll see," he promised, stroking her hair. "There's got to be one out there, and I'll dig him out."

Somehow.

Faint light had barely streaked over the horizon when Jess carefully slipped out of Nick's bed. He was finally sleeping soundly, and she didn't want to waken him.

She borrowed his robe from the closet and put it on, then padded out into the kitchen. She set up the coffee machine and sat at the kitchen table while waiting for it to heat.

Darn him, she thought. He was in trouble, and she wanted so much to help him. Why couldn't he see that she would only be an investor? Why couldn't she get that through his thick pride? Grateful as she was that his business wasn't on the stock exchange, she still couldn't help wishing that it was. It would be so easy then. She'd be one of the nameless out there who put her money into his stocks. He wouldn't even think twice about it then.

She had to help him somehow. She couldn't stand by while he was ruined because of his stubborn pride. There were times when a person absolutely needed help, and this was one of them.

But how?

The coffee machine sputtered, signaling the last of the water going through the system. With a sigh, Jess got up and began to walk to the other end of the counter. She passed the telephone hanging on the wall.

She walked backward to it and picked up the receiver. She punched out a number. It rang twice before a deep voice rumbled, "Hello."

"Dad? I'm sorry it's so early, but I need your help."

Thirteen

Two days later Nick watched his men as they worked on the other two houses, readying them for occupancy. He must have been crazy to listen to Jess, he thought. But she'd been so confident he would find a new backer that he had been convinced to reopen the site. He had spent the last couple of days looking for one everywhere, short of overturning rocks. He'd rather be bankrupt and out of business before he sought that kind of money. Unfortunately, at the moment it seemed to be the only money available.

Tommy had received his check yesterday, he thought dismally. And tomorrow was payday for the men. If anyone ever wanted to know how to commit business suicide, he could certainly tell them.

"How did it go?" Jess asked from behind him.

He turned around and smiled in apology. He hadn't even heard her. Loosening his tie, he said, "The banks were interested, but they want to wait until they see what the market will do. Everyone has said that so far."

She sighed. "You've got some telephone messages. Go see."

"You're supposed to be landscaping," he said sternly.

She pointed to the busy construction workers. "Sam doesn't have the time to answer the phone right now." She smiled. "Besides, that damn thing rings all over the site, and it drives me crazy. Tony called." She hesitated for a moment. "I hope I wasn't overstepping boundaries . . . but I told him."

"I'm glad," he said, walking toward the office. "Frankly, I've been avoiding it. It's a good thing I have a smart brother who won't listen to me. He'll need that job now. I certainly couldn't pay for law school."

Jess chuckled. "That's exactly what Tony said."

Nick smiled wryly. "Maybe Tony could get me a job with the show. Think I'd make it as a male stripper?"

"Absolutely." She linked her arm through his. "But I won't let you."

"I don't know, Jess," he teased. "According to Tony, the pay is terrific."

"You can strip for me personally," she said in a low voice. "My pay is better."

"Very true."

In the office, he looked through the messages. One instantly caught his eye. It was from Tommy Sayers's banker, asking that he return the call immediately.

"This is from the banker who came with Tommy," he said to Jess, who had followed him into the office. "I wonder what he wants."

She shrugged. "You won't know until you call him back. He did say it was very important."

"Yes, but . . ." *Oh, Lord*, he thought. If there was a problem with the check . . .

The secretary put him straight through. Nick's stomach churned and sweat beaded his forehead as the banker greeted him.

"I'll come right to the point," the man said. "I received a call from someone I know at Standard Associates. He's looking for a good solid investment in properties right now, and I instantly thought of you."

Nick's heart seemed to stop beating, then suddenly thumped painfully in his chest. He glanced across the desk at Jess. It was obvious she could sense his excitement. Her eyes were glittering, and she was breathing heavily as she leaned forward in the chair.

"I see," Nick said, surprised at the calm coolness of his voice.

"I gave him the particulars, knowing them from Mr. Sayers. He said it sounded exactly like what he was looking for, and he wants very much to get it on the project. I, of course, couldn't give him a figure—"

Nick wanted to yell at the man that he could have given Tommy's investment costs. The idiot knew that too.

"—but he did name about how much he was looking to put in. I can assure you that you'll be pleased."

Nick let his breath out in a rush.

"That sounds promising," he said. *Never let them know you're sweating*, he thought. "But I am looking for a good solid investor . . . ."

"Then this is your man," the banker hastened to

assure him. "George Carlson is the president of Standard Associates, a fine businessman, absolutely rock solid."

Nick had heard of Standard Associates, and he wanted badly to grin. But he had one last question. The biggie. "When is Mr. Carlson looking to do this?"

"As soon as possible. He has some windfall profits from another project that he needs to invest immediately. He can have it to you by close of business today, if you like."

"But doesn't he want to sign a contract first?" Nick asked, surprised that the man was so quick to get his money in.

"George is a very old-fashioned businessman," the banker said. "He believes in reputation, and he was already aware of yours. He trusts his own judgment implicitly, and, I'm honored to say, mine. He also feels that if a man will renege on a deal, he'll do it with or without a contract, and I suppose that's true to a certain degree. I think you'll find him rather interesting."

"I'm sure I will," Nick agreed. Not only that, he'd kiss the man's feet, and the banker's too. "Thank you very much for thinking of me, sir."

"I was glad to do it, Mr. Mikaris. I was quite bothered by what happened with Mr. Sayers. So foolish. Unfortunately, he's paying for it now."

After he said good-bye, Nick set the receiver gently on its cradle. Then he burst from the chair.

"Yahooo!"

"What?" Jess asked, jumping up. "Was it a backer?"

"A wonderful backer!" Nick shouted, hurrying around the desk and pulling her into his arms. He swung her around. "George Carlson from Standard

Associates, and he wants to invest in MeadowHill right away. Today. We're back in business, Jess!"

"I knew it! I just knew it!" She was grinning and hugging him. "I'm so glad for you, Nick."

"I'm so glad for me, too." In between his chatter of excitement, he hugged and kissed her repeatedly.

When their initial exhilaration finally subsided, he pressed her closer. "Let's celebrate. Here. Now."

"Nick!"

He kissed the pulse point just under her ear. She shivered. He wanted her so badly. "We haven't made love for a while."

"You've been worried and upset."

"I'm not now." He smoothed his hands down her back and cupped her bottom.

"Nick, we can't!" Her eyes were wide with shock at his suggestion. "We're in the office."

"So?" He grinned as he frogmarched her backward to the door. Reaching over, he snapped the lock shut. "Now we have privacy."

She struggled in his tight embrace. "I'm all covered with dirt and I look like a slob!"

"You have no idea how much your worn jeans and ripped-up sweatsuit jacket have driven me crazy." He strung kisses down her neck. "Every day you look so damn sexy, and I can never touch you for fear I'll take you on the spot and to hell with whoever's there."

She arched her neck back, allowing him further access, while she whispered, "There's no bed, no couch."

He smiled against her warm soft flesh as he unzipped her ratty jacket. He pressed her against the wall.

"We don't need one."

Tuesday morning, Jess finally allowed herself to breathe a huge sigh of relief. The money had been transferred. The new "backer" had visited the site, and the contracts had been duly signed and sealed. Mikaris Builders was back in business for good.

And she didn't feel an ounce of guilt that the money sitting happily in the MeadowHill account was actually hers.

In truth, she had made a good investment, and that was all she had done. Okay, so she had had to be devious, but that was because Nick had been foolishly stubborn and macho about the whole thing. Fortunately, he'd never know she was the real investor.

She hid a smile as she remembered her father's telling her that George Carlson had refused to be her front man until he had checked out Nick's business credentials. She had thought she'd go crazy before the man was finally satisfied and had made the call. And her father had been no better, she admitted in amused frustration. Devlin Brannen had insisted on being satisfied that Carlson was satisfied.

"She's off in space again."

She glanced up to find Duane grinning at her.

Roger chuckled. "If she isn't off in space, then she's with Mikaris."

Jess smiled. "Get to work, guys. We've got sod to lay."

Roger grinned. "I do love this job. It's got sexy words—"

"Now who's that?" Duane interrupted, pointing toward the office.

Jess turned around to see Tony Mikaris climb out of a battered MG. "That's Nick's brother. But he's supposed to be at school."

"I thought he was one of those strippers," Roger said, frowning.

"How do you know that?" Jess asked, surprised.

"The guys here know about it. They told us. Hard to believe Mikaris has a brother like that."

"He doesn't look like much," Duane commented, in a snide tone.

"Yeah," Roger agreed. "Don't know why the women go bonkers over him."

"And I don't know why only the female of the species is accused of cattiness," Jess said.

Tony spotted her and waved. She waved back and walked over to greet him.

"Don't you have school?" she asked, after saying hello.

"I took the day off. I thought I'd better come and see Nick. How's Cat?"

She moaned. "Please, Tony. Don't even tease about that."

Tony laughed. "You're doing okay?"

She nodded.

Duane and Roger might not know why the ladies went crazy for Tony, but she did. He had a caring quality in him that touched the heart of a woman— just as Nick had. Also, she thought with amusement, she'd seen the show.

When Nick joined them, Jess started to excuse herself, but he stopped her.

"Stay, Jess. You're family."

She was pleased, but she couldn't help feeling like a puppy at the command. She definitely needed to work on Nick.

Tony glanced at her, then said, "I'm quitting law school."

"What?" Nick shouted.

"Tony, you can't!" Jess exclaimed.

"I can." Tony stared at his brother. "I've thought about it over the last couple of days. I hated it that you were in trouble and I wasn't helping you."

Nick's face was turning a dull dark red. "And how could you have helped?"

"I could have been in the business with you," Tony said, pointing a finger at his brother. "I could have shouldered the worry, helped you find a backer. You shouldn't have been in it alone, Nick."

"I found a backer. Dammit, I called you and told you that! Everything's settled. There's no way you could have helped, Tony."

"But I've been selfish, giving you a hard time about the way I'm paying for school." Tony put his hand on Nick's shoulder. "No, it's time I made Mikaris Builders a family business. Admit it, Nick, you'd really like that."

Nick shook his hand off. "I don't want you in the business. I never have. All I ever wanted for you was to do exactly what you're doing. You'll stay in school and that's final!"

"But I don't want you worrying any longer about how I'm paying for it," Tony protested. "You've done so much for me and—"

Nick didn't let him finish. Jess held her breath at

the explosion, glad that it wasn't directed at her. His anger was almost frightening. Tony kept silent.

". . . and, dammit, Tony, you are staying in school if I have to drag you there," Nick went on, waving his arms. "I won't say a word if you take your clothes off for a thousand women, okay? As long as it's just to pay for school! But you stay in and become a lawyer. It's what I really want."

"Well, I'd feel better if I knew you wanted me to keep the job."

"Hell, yes," Nick said vehemently, calming down slightly. "I just said it, didn't I? To tell you the truth, not having to worry about paying for your schooling was the only plus in the whole mess last week. I could think of a lot worse things for you, and believe me, working as a male stripper to pay for law school isn't one of them!"

Suddenly Jess realized exactly what Tony was doing. She swallowed heavily to keep from laughing.

"I want you back at school this afternoon," Nick ordered. "That lousy cement mixer we rented is churning out garbage, so I'm going into the office to call the leasing company. When I come out, I expect you to be on the turnpike, heading back to New York."

"Yes, Nick," Tony said meekly.

"Good." Nick stomped off to the trailer and slammed the door shut behind him.

"You stinker!" Jess said, keeping her voice low.

"And in front of a witness," Tony said with satisfaction. "You heard him. I pay for school myself."

"I can't believe you would sucker Nick into saying that." Although it had been funny at the time, now her anger was building at Tony's deviousness. "That was one of the rottenest—"

"I meant it, Jess." Tony met her gaze squarely. "About going into the business with him. Everything I said was what I'd thought about all weekend, and if he had wanted me in the business then I would have done it. I owe him a lot."

"But you were hoping he'd do exactly what he did."

Tony grinned. "I admit that it was the perfect opportunity to finally settle this between us. Sometimes you have to take my bullheaded brother by the horns and swing him around in your direction."

Jess sighed in defeat. She knew exactly how stubborn Nick could be. "But I will tell you, Tony Mikaris, that your exams had better be spotless, or you'll have me to deal with."

A worried look came into Tony's eyes. "Are you going to be worse than Nick?"

"Infinitely."

Tony groaned.

"So we're back in business," Sandy said that afternoon.

"Yes." Jess smiled as she watched Nick walking over to where she and Sandy stood in the driveway of the model home. There was a spring to his step, and she knew what had put it there. Lunch had been extremely satisfactory, she thought. But they'd better not have another "private picnic" while on the job. It was much too easy to stay away.

"Good," Sandy said, "because you and Nick need to go look at bedroom furniture."

"Bedroom furniture?" Nick asked, having heard the last words. "Of course, Jess and I will look for bedroom furniture. I guarantee we'll do an exhaustive search."

Jess lightly punched his arm. "Nick!"

Sandy laughed. "Maybe Marty and I ought to do it. You know, married life and all."

"Forget it," Nick said. "We got the job first."

"That's what counts." Sandy smiled at him. "Ever since I started helping with the decorating, I feel like I have a major stake in this project. So may I ask who the backer is?"

Jess suddenly had a queasy feeling in her stomach. She and Sandy had been best friends since childhood. They knew a lot about each other's families. Sandy was one area she'd forgotten about in her cover-up.

"We really should get back to work," she said brightly, before Nick could open his mouth.

"Sure, Jess," Sandy said, then turned back to Nick. "So who?"

"Carlson of Standard Associates—" Nick began.

"Sandy, we have to get back to work!" Jess said with as much sternness as she could muster. Walking toward the house, she prayed Sandy would follow. She was afraid to "help" her friend along. Nick might realize she was trying to keep Sandy from talking further to him.

To Jess's immense relief, Sandy began to follow. But she kept talking to Nick over her shoulder. "The slave driver calls. But it's great news, Nick. Especially about this guy from Standard Associates. Jess has a good connection there, you know. Her father's on the board of directors."

The words were like a death knell vibrating through Jess's entire body. She began walking faster. Maybe Nick wouldn't pick up on—

"Jess!"

Her name literally roared through the construction site. She halted instantly and spun around.

"Uh-oh," Sandy muttered.

"Dammit!" Nick cried as he strode toward her. His voice rose in volume. "Dammit, Jess! Carlson didn't call out of the blue, did he? You got him to help me, didn't you?"

"Nick, please, calm down," she began in placating tones.

"The hell I'll calm down!" His face was even redder than it had been that morning with Tony. "You tell Carlson he's getting his money back right now! I want a legitimate backer, not some clown you arm-twisted into helping out!"

"It's my money, dammit, and it's staying put!" she shouted back.

"*Your* money?"

Jess had thought he was angry before, but right at that moment she considered it a miracle of control that he didn't kill her. And if he tried, she thought murderously, she'd take him apart. She lifted her chin in clear defiance.

Nick finally found his voice. "You'll have *your* money back within the hour!"

She glared at him. "You can't do that! Everybody will lose their jobs again! They can't afford that, and neither can you!"

"I'll find another backer to take your place!" he yelled, despite them being almost nose to nose.

"No, you won't!" she yelled in return. "And you jolly well know it!"

"You're fired!"

"No, I'm not! Not only am I doing the landscaping, but I'm doing the decorating, too. You can't afford to lose me now. I'm an investor in this project, and I say I stay. Right, Sandy?"

"Oh . . . ah . . ." Sandy had backed out of firing range. "Right."

"I don't want your money!" Nick roared. "Why can't you understand that?"

"Why can't you understand that I'm simply an investor?" she demanded. "I've found a great place to put some money and make even more out of it. It's strictly business! Right, Sandy?"

"Right." The reply came from a good twenty feet away.

Nick straightened and said coldly, "You warned me, Jess. You said you would hurt me, and I didn't believe you. I didn't think there was anything you could do that would drive me away. I was wrong."

"This doesn't count!" she screamed, desperate to correct him. "I told you I do it without knowing I'm doing it. I knew exactly what I was doing—"

"What do you mean, it doesn't count!" The shouting match suddenly rose in pitch. "I told you No, and you deliberately disregarded me!"

"And wouldn't you have done the same thing if the situation were reversed?" She shook her fist in his face. "You know you would have jumped right in, like I did."

"This," he said righteously, "is entirely different."

"Bull!" He was being so obtuse she wanted to shake him. "If I didn't think these homes would sell, then I wouldn't have put my money into them. I would have tried to talk you out of continuing. I'm an investor, pure and simple! How many times do I have to tell you that before it gets through your stupid pride?"

"It's not pride!"

"Then what is it?"

"I love you, Jess, not your money!"

Suddenly, she realized that she was fighting for him. For him, not against him. The smothering panic was gone, totally and completely. In fact, it hadn't been there for a long time now. But she and Nick were at a stalemate, both of them on the verge of destroying the relationship. She had to find some solution . . . .

"You're marrying me," she announced, and was immediately shocked at the notion.

"Marry!"

The stunned expression on Nick's face matched her own. Still, Jess knew she was doing exactly the right thing. For more than one reason.

"Husbands and wives are business partners all the time," she said, taking the bull by the horns and steering him in the right direction. "After we're married, then I'll be your partner in business . . . and in love. Surely, you can't object to that."

"Dammit, Jess!"

"Oh, be quiet, Nick." She grinned at him, knowing he was near defeat. Not a single one of his objections had been logical, and he had to have realized it. She had saved her best ammunition for last. "I love you, Nick. I've never loved anyone the way I love you, and I never will. We're getting married and that's final. Right, Sandy?"

"Right!" Sandy yelled from across the lawn.

Nick stared at her.

She stared back.

"Dammit, Jess," he said again, but quietly this time. He glared at her for a moment longer, then pulled her into his arms. His mouth found hers instantly.

Jess clung to him tightly. Her mind registered the loud cheer from all the men, but she didn't pay any attention to it. She was getting married.

For the last time in her life.

Epilogue

She had him wrapped around her little finger . . . and he didn't give a damn, Nick thought happily as he opened the door to the model house for Jess.

She smiled at him before stepping inside. "I can't believe it's finished."

"It's a home," he said, kissing her gently.

Their footsteps echoed hollowly on the oak parquet floor of the foyer. It was amazing how silent the site was on a Sunday afternoon, he thought. No hammering, no machinery deafening the ears. Nothing.

In the next second, shouts of "Surprise!" blasted through the air. Nick grinned as Jess shrieked and jumped back against him.

People crowded around them, laughing and talking all at once. Sandy was in the forefront.

"What's going on?" Jess cried.

"It's your bridal shower, you dope!" Sandy said.

"That's my woman you're talking about," Nick said sternly, then laughed.

Jess gave him a look as she was pulled away and into the living room. He knew what it meant: She'd kill him for getting her here with a very suggestive promise. He grinned. It was a little bit of revenge for her outrageous proposal. A proposal that had stopped him in his rantings, a proposal that had left him helpless and exhilarated. She had taken him completely by surprise. He had realized he'd been about to push her away forever. He could have survived any disaster but that.

In the kitchen he found Tony and Marty. He shed his jacket, then helped them ready food and drinks. Sandy had managed to wrangle the three of them into playing waiters.

"You didn't forget the package, I hope," he said to Tony.

"Of course not," Tony said, pointing at a gaily wrapped box sitting in an out-of-the-way corner.

Nick went over and opened the lid. The contents were a little frayed around the edges, and he sighed, straightening them as best he could.

"Jess is going to strangle you, you know," Tony said.

"Probably," he agreed. "Well, we'll just have to have the wedding in her prison cell."

"Or at your funeral," Marty said.

Nick waited until the end of the present-opening, then tucked one more gift in the box and carried it carefully out into the living room. He set it on Jess's lap. She was wearing a paper plate hat covered with bows and ribbons. She looked tired and happy and ridiculous and beautiful. Tony and Marty watched from the doorway, both of them grinning widely.

"Open it," Nick said.

Jess looked up at him and smiled, then opened the box. When she saw the contents, she glanced sharply at the other men.

Grinning in immense satisfaction, Nick said, "Meet Cat."

"You knew." She drew the words out as she deliberately set the box on the floor and slowly rose from the chair. Nick backed away from the flare of anger in her dark eyes.

"Now, Jess . . ."

"You knew all this time!" she said, advancing toward him. The guests in the room were silent, avidly watching. "Do you know how sick I've been over not telling you that was Tony in the bathroom? I made a complete and total idiot of myself that night!"

"I know," he said.

Sensibly, he grabbed her and kissed her soundly. She melted against him, and he decided the finger-winding worked both ways.

"I'll take her back," he murmured when he finally lifted his head.

"The hell you will!" She scrambled out of his arms and hurried back to the box. Lifting out the bundle of orange and white fur, she cuddled the kitten against her chest. Cat squirmed against her, and Jess pulled the heavy paper out of the shredded ribbon tied around the animal's neck. She unfolded it and stared at the writing.

"It's a deed!" she exclaimed. "For this house! Nick, you bought the model!"

She practically flew into his arms this time, kitten and all. He pressed her tightly to him. The kitten mewed in protest.

"You made it a home, Jess. Our home."

"I love you," she whispered.

"You may not when you realize we can't move in until after we're done using it as a model."

"It'll sell the rest of MeadowHill in a week."

"Will you two hurry up with the mushy stuff?" Sandy said, walking over to the stereo. "We want the entertainment."

"Here!" Jess thrust the kitten and the deed into Nick's hands. "Get the camera, Mom!"

Jess's mother, whom Nick had met shortly after their engagement and immediately liked, was pushing wrapping paper aside in an attempt to find the camera. He watched in bewilderment as she and Jess grabbed for it at the same time. Jess won.

"I got it!"

"Right," Sandy said, and flipped on the tape deck. "Let's Get Physical" blared from the speakers.

Marty suddenly shouted, "Ohmigod!"

Nick turned around to discover his brother rotating his hips and unbuttoning his shirtcuffs.

"Tony!" he exclaimed in horror.

Jess started snapping pictures.

"Jess!" he exclaimed in more horror.

Jess's mother came over to him. Her face was bright red, and she was laughing. She took the kitten from him and said, "It's all in the family, Nicolas."

"She's going to drive me crazy for the rest of my life," he said, and grinned.

THE EDITOR'S CORNER

What a wonderful summer of romance reading we have in store for you. Truly, you're going to be LOVESWEPT with some happy surprises through the long, hot, lazy days ahead.

First, you're going to get **POCKETS FULL OF JOY**, LOVESWEPT #270, by our new Canadian author, Judy Gill. Elaina McIvor wondered helplessly what she was going to do with an eleven-month-old baby to care for. Dr. "Brad" Bradshaw had been the stork and deposited the infant on her doorstep and raced away. But he was back soon enough to "play doctor" and "play house" in one of the most delightful and sensuous romances of the season.

Joan Elliott Pickart has created two of her most intriguing characters ever in **TATTERED WINGS**, LOVESWEPT #271. Devastatingly handsome Mark Hampton—an Air Force Colonel whose once exciting life now seems terribly lonely—and beautiful, enigmatic Eden Landry—a top fashion model who left her glamorous life for a secluded ranch—meet one snowy night. Desire flares immediately. But so do problems. Mark soon discovers that Eden is like a perfect butterfly encased in a cube of glass. You'll revel in the ways he finds to break down the walls without hurting the woman!

For all of you who've written to ask for Tara's and Jed's love story, here your fervent requests

(continued)

are answered with Barbara Boswell's terrific **AND TARA, TOO,** LOVESWEPT #272. As we know, Jed Ramsey is as darkly sleek and as seductive and as winning with women as a man can be. And Tara Brady wants no part of him. It would be just too convenient, she thinks, if all the Brady sisters married Ramsey men. But that's exactly what Jed's tyrannical father has in mind. You'll chuckle and gasp as Tara and Jed rattle the chains of fate in a breathlessly sensual and touching love story.

Margie McDonnell is an author who can transport you to another world. This time she takes you to **THE LAND OF ENCHANTMENT,** via LOVE-SWEPT #273, to meet a modern-day, ever so gallant knight, dashing Patrick Knight, and the sensitive and lovely Karen Harris. Karen is the single parent of an exceptional son and a quite sensible lady . . . until she falls for the handsome hunk who is as merry as he is creative. We think you'll delight in this very special, very thrilling love story.

It gives us enormous pleasure next month to celebrate the fifth anniversary of Iris Johansen's writing career. Her first ever published book was LOVESWEPT's **STORMY VOWS** in August 1983. With that and its companion romance **TEMPEST AT SEA,** published in September 1983, Iris launched the romance featuring spin-off and/or continuing characters. Now everyone's doing it! But, still,

(continued)

nobody does it quite like the woman who began it all, Iris Johansen. Here, next month, you'll meet old friends and new lovers in **BLUE SKIES AND SHINING PROMISES**, LOVESWEPT #274. (The following month she'll also have a LOVESWEPT, of course, and we wonder if you can guess who the featured characters will be.) Don't miss the thrilling love story of Cameron Bandor (yes, you know him) and Damita Shaughnessy, whose background will shock, surprise and move you, taking you right back to five years ago!

Welcome, back, Peggy Webb! In the utterly bewitching LOVESWEPT #275, **SLEEPLESS NIGHTS,** Peggy tells the story of Tanner Donovan of the quicksilver eyes and Amanda Lassiter of the tart tongue and tender heart. In this thrilling and sensuous story, you have a marvelous battle of wits between lovers parted in the past and determined to best each other in the present. A real delight!

As always, we hope that not one of our LOVE-SWEPTs will ever disappoint you. Enjoy!

Carolyn Nichols

Carolyn Nichols
   Editor
LOVESWEPT
Bantam Books
666 Fifth Avenue
New York, NY 10103

THE HOMETOWN HUNK CONTEST

FOR EVERY WOMAN WHO HAS EVER SAID—
"I know a man who looks just like the hero of this book"
—HAVE WE GOT A CONTEST FOR YOU!

To help celebrate our fifth year of publishing LOVESWEPT we are having a fabulous, fun-filled event called THE HOMETOWN HUNK contest. We are going to reissue six classic early titles by six of your favorite authors.

DARLING OBSTACLES by Barbara Boswell
IN A CLASS BY ITSELF by Sandra Brown
C.J.'S FATE by Kay Hooper
THE LADY AND THE UNICORN by Iris Johansen
CHARADE by Joan Elliott Pickart
FOR THE LOVE OF SAMI by Fayrene Preston

Here, as in the backs of all July, August, and September 1988 LOVESWEPTS you will find "cover notes" just like the ones we prepare at Bantam as the background for our art director to create our covers. These notes will describe the hero and heroine, give a teaser on the plot, and suggest a scene for the cover. Your part in the contest will be to see if a great looking local man—or men, if your hometown is so blessed—fits our description of one of the heroes of the six books we will reissue.

THE HOMETOWN HUNK who is selected (one for each of the six titles) will be flown to New York via United Airlines and will stay at the Loews Summit Hotel—the ideal hotel for business or pleasure in midtown Manhattan—for two nights. All travel arrangements made by Reliable Travel International, Incorporated. He will be the model for the new cover of the book which will be released in mid-1989. The six people who send in the winning photos of their HOMETOWN HUNK will receive a pre-selected assortment of LOVESWEPT books free for one year. Please see the Official Rules above the Official Entry Form for full details and restrictions.

We can't wait to start judging those pictures! Oh, and you must let the man you've chosen know that you're entering him in the contest. After all, if he wins he'll have to come to New York.

Have fun. Here's your chance to get the cover-lover of your dreams!

Carolyn Nichols

Carolyn Nichols
Editor
LOVESWEPT
Bantam Books
666 Fifth Avenue
New York, NY 10102—0023

THE HOMETOWN HUNK CONTEST

DARLING OBSTACLES
(Originally Published as LOVESWEPT #95)
By Barbara Boswell

COVER NOTES

The Characters:

Hero:
GREG WILDER's gorgeous body and "to-die-for" good looks
haven't hurt him in the dating department, but when
most women discover he's a widower with four kids, they
head for the hills! Greg has the hard, muscular build of an
athlete, and his light brown hair, which he wears neatly
parted on the side, is streaked blond by the sun. Add to
that his aquamarine blue eyes that sparkle when he laughs,
and his sensual mouth and generous lower lip, and you're
probably wondering what woman in her right mind
wouldn't want Greg's strong, capable surgeon's hands working their magic on her—kids or no kids!

Personality Traits:
An acclaimed neurosurgeon, Greg Wilder is a celebrity of
sorts in the planned community of Woodland, Maryland.
Authoritative, debonair, self-confident, his reputation for
engaging in one casual relationship after another almost
overshadows his prowess as a doctor. In reality, Greg
dates more out of necessity than anything else, since he
has to attend one social function after another. He con-
siders most of the events boring and wishes he could
spend more time with his children. But his profession is a
difficult and demanding one—and being both father and
mother to four kids isn't any less so. A thoughtful, generous, sometimes befuddled father, Greg tries to do it all.
Cerebral, he uses his intellect and skill rather than physical
strength to win his victories. However, he never expected
to come up against one Mary Magdalene May!

Heroine:
MARY MAGDALENE MAY, called Maggie by her friends, is the thirty-two-year-old mother of three children. She has shoulder-length auburn hair, and green eyes that shout her Irish heritage. With high cheekbones and an upturned nose covered with a smattering of freckles, Maggie thinks of herself more as the girl-next-door type. Certainly, she believes, she could never be one of Greg Wilder's beautiful escorts.

Setting: The small town of Woodland, Maryland

The Story:
Surgeon Greg Wilder wanted to court the feisty and beautiful widow who'd been caring for his four kids, but she just wouldn't let him past her doorstep! Sure that his interest was only casual, and that he preferred more sophisticated women, Maggie May vowed to keep Greg at arm's length. But he wouldn't take no for an answer. And once he'd crashed through her defenses and pulled her into his arms, he was tireless—and reckless—in his campaign to win her over. Maggie had found it tough enough to resist one determined doctor; now he threatened to call in his kids and hers as reinforcements—seven rowdy snags to romance!

Cover scene:
As if romancing Maggie weren't hard enough, Greg can't seem to find time to spend with her without their children around. Stealing a private moment on the stairs in Maggie's house, Greg and Maggie embrace. She is standing one step above him, but she still has to look up at him to see into his eyes. Greg's hands are on her hips, and her hands are resting on his shoulders. Maggie is wearing a very sheer, short pink nightgown, and Greg has on wheat-colored jeans and a navy and yellow striped rugby shirt. Do they have time to kiss?

THE HOMETOWN HUNK CONTEST

IN A CLASS BY ITSELF
(Originally Published as LOVESWEPT #66)
By Sandra Brown

COVER NOTES

The Characters:

Hero:
LOGAN WEBSTER would have no trouble posing for a
Scandinavian travel poster. His wheat-colored hair always
seems to be tousled, defying attempts to control it, and
falls across his wide forehead. Thick eyebrows one shade
darker than his hair accentuate his crystal blue eyes. He
has a slender nose that flairs slightly over a mouth that
testifies to both sensitivity and strength. The faint lines
around his eyes and alongside his mouth give the impression that reaching the ripe age of 30 wasn't all fun and
games for him. Logan's square, determined jaw is punctu-
ated by a vertical cleft. His broad shoulders and narrow
waist add to his tall, lean appearance.

Personality traits:
Logan Webster has had to scrape and save and fight for
everything he's gotten. Born into a poor farm family, he
was driven to succeed and overcome his "wrong side of
the tracks" image. His businesses include cattle, real estate, and natural gas. Now a pillar of the community,
Logan's life has been a true rags-to-riches story. Only
Sandra Brown's own words can describe why he is masculinity epitomized: "Logan had 'the walk,' that saddle-
tramp saunter that was inherent to native Texan men,
passed down through generations of cowboys. It was, without even trying to be, sexy. The unconscious roll of the
hips, the slow strut, the flexed knees, the slouching stance,
the deceptive laziness that hid a latent aggressiveness."
Wow! And not only does he have "the walk," but he's fun

and generous and kind. Even with his wealth, he feels at home living in his small hometown with simple, hardworking, middle-class, backbone-of-America folks. A born leader, people automatically gravitate toward him.

Heroine:
DANI QUINN is a sophisticated twenty-eight-year-old woman. Dainty, her body compact, she is utterly feminine. Dani's pale, lustrous hair is moonlight and honey spun together, and because it is very straight, she usually wears it in a chignon. With golden eyes to match her golden hair, Dani is the one woman Logan hasn't been able to get off his mind for the ten years they've been apart.

Setting: Primarily on Logan's ranch in East Texas.

The Story:
Ten years had passed since Dani Quinn had graduated from high school in the small Texas town, ten years since the night her elopement with Logan Webster had ended in disaster. Now Dani approached her tenth reunion with uncertainty. Logan would be there . . . Logan, the only man who'd ever made her shiver with desire and need, but would she have the courage to face the fury in his eyes? She couldn't defend herself against his anger and hurt—to do so would demand she reveal the secret sorrow she shared with no one. Logan's touch had made her his so long ago. Could he reach past the pain to make her his for all time?

Cover Scene:
It's sunset, and Logan and Dani are standing beside the swimming pool on his ranch, embracing. The pool is surrounded by semitropical plants and lush flower beds. In the distance, acres of rolling pasture land resembling a green lake undulate into dense, piney woods. Dani is wearing a strapless, peacock blue bikini and sandals with leather ties that wrap around her ankles. Her hair is straight and loose, falling to the middle of her back. Logan has on a light-colored pair of corduroy shorts and a short-sleeved designer knit shirt in a pale shade of yellow.

THE HOMETOWN HUNK CONTEST

C.J.'S FATE
(Originally Published as LOVESWEPT #32)
By Kay Hooper

COVER NOTES

The Characters:

Hero:
FATE WESTON easily could have walked straight off an Indian reservation. His raven black hair and strong, well-molded features testify to his heritage. But somewhere along the line genetics threw Fate a curve—his eyes are the deepest, darkest blue imaginable! Above those blue eyes are dark slanted eyebrows, and fanning out from those eyes are faint laugh lines—the only sign of the fact that he's thirty-four years old. Tall, Fate moves with easy, loose-limbed grace. Although he isn't an athlete, Fate takes very good care of himself, and it shows in his strong physique. Striking at first glance and fascinating with each succeeding glance, the serious expressions on his face make him look older than his years, but with one smile he looks boyish again.

Personality traits:
Fate possesses a keen sense of humor. His heavy-lidded, intelligent eyes are capable of concealment, but there is a shrewdness in them that reveals the man hadn't needed college or a law degree to be considered intelligent. The set of his head tells you that he is proud—perhaps even a bit arrogant. He is attractive and perfectly well aware of that fact. Unconventional, paradoxical, tender, silly, lusty, gentle, comical, serious, absurd, and endearing are all words that come to mind when you think of Fate. He is not ashamed to be everything a man can be. A defense attorney by profession, one can detect a bit of frustrated actor in his character. More than anything else, though, it's the

impression of humor about him—reinforced by the elusive dimple in his cheek—that makes Fate Weston a scrumptious hero!

Heroine:
C.J. ADAMS is a twenty-six-year-old research librarian. Unaware of her own attractiveness, C.J. tends to play down her pixylike figure and tawny gold eyes. But once she meets Fate, she no longer feels that her short, burnished copper curls and the sprinkling of freckles on her nose make her unappealing. He brings out the vixen in her, and changes the smart, bookish woman who professed to have no interest in men into the beautiful, sexy woman she really was all along. Now, if only he could get her to tell him what C.J. stands for!

Setting: Ski lodge in Aspen, Colorado

The Story:
C.J. Adams had been teased enough about her seeming lack of interest in the opposite sex. On a ski trip with her five best friends, she impulsively embraced a handsome stranger, pretending they were secret lovers—and the delighted lawyer who joined in her impetuous charade seized the moment to deepen the kiss. Astonished at his reaction, C.J. tried to nip their romance in the bud—but found herself nipping at his neck instead! She had met her match in a man who could answer her witty remarks with clever ripostes of his own, and a lover whose caresses aroused in her a passionate need she'd never suspected that she could feel. Had destiny somehow tossed them together?

Cover Scene:
C.J. and Fate virtually have the ski slopes to themselves early one morning, and they take advantage of it! Frolicking in a snow drift, Fate is covering C.J. with snow—and kisses! They are flushed from the cold weather and from the excitement of being in love. C.J. is wearing a sky-blue, one-piece, tight-fitting ski outfit that zips down the front. Fate is wearing a navy blue parka and matching ski pants.

THE HOMETOWN HUNK CONTEST

THE LADY AND THE UNICORN
(Originally Published as LOVESWEPT #29)
By Iris Johansen

COVER NOTES

The Characters:

Hero:
Not classically handsome, RAFE SANTINE's blunt, craggy features reinforce the quality of overpowering virility about him. He has wide, Slavic cheekbones and a bold, thrusting chin, which give the impression of strength and authority. Thick black eyebrows are set over piercing dark eyes. He wears his heavy, dark hair long. His large frame measures in at almost six feet four inches, and it's hard to believe that a man with such brawny shoulders and strong thighs could exhibit the pantherlike grace which characterizes Rafe's movements. Rafe Santine is definitely a man to be reckoned with, and heroine Janna Cannon does just that!

Personality traits:
Our hero is a man who radiates an aura of power and danger, and women find him intriguing and irresistible. Rafe Santine is a self-made billionaire at the age of thirty-eight. Almost entirely self-educated, he left school at sixteen to work on his first construction job, and by the time he was twenty-three, he owned the company. From there he branched out into real estate, computers, and oil. Rafe reportedly changes mistresses as often as he changes shirts. His reputation for ruthless brilliance has been earned over years of fighting to the top of the economic ladder from the slums of New York. His gruff manner and hard personality hide the tender, vulnerable side of him. Rafe also possesses an insatiable thirst for knowledge that is a passion with him. Oddly enough, he has a wry sense of

humor that surfaces unexpectedly from time to time. And, though cynical to the extreme, he never lets his natural skepticism interfere with his innate sense of justice.

Heroine:
JANNA CANNON, a game warden for a small wildlife preserve, is a very dedicated lady. She is tall at five feet nine inches and carries herself in a stately way. Her long hair is dark brown and is usually twisted into a single thick braid in back. Of course, Rafe never lets her keep her hair braided when they make love! Janna is one quarter Cherokee Indian by heritage, and she possesses the dark eyes and skin of her ancestors.

Setting: Rafe's estate in Carmel, California

The Story:
Janna Cannon scaled the high walls of Rafe Santine's private estate, afraid of nothing and determined to appeal to the powerful man who could save her beloved animal preserve. She bewitched his guard dogs, then cast a spell of enchantment over him as well. Janna's profound grace, her caring nature, made the tough and proud Rafe grow mercurial in her presence. She offered him a gift he'd never risked reaching out for before—but could he trust his own emotions enough to open himself to her love?

Cover Scene:
In the gazebo overlooking the rugged cliffs at the edge of the Pacific Ocean, Rafe and Janna share a passionate moment together. The gazebo is made of redwood and the interior is small and cozy. Scarlet cushions cover the benches, and matching scarlet curtains hang from the eaves, caught back by tasseled sashes to permit the sea breeze to whip through the enclosure. Rafe is wearing black suede pants and a charcoal gray crew-neck sweater. Janna is wearing a safari-style khaki shirt-and-slacks outfit and suede desert boots. They embrace against the breathtaking backdrop of wild, crashing, white-crested waves pounding the rocks and cliffs below.

THE HOMETOWN HUNK CONTEST

CHARADE
(Originally Published as LOVESWEPT #74)
By Joan Elliott Pickart

COVER NOTES

The Characters:

Hero:
The phrase tall, dark, and handsome was coined to describe TENNES WHITNEY. His coal black hair reaches past his collar in back, and his fathomless steel gray eyes are framed by the kind of thick, dark lashes that a woman would kill to have. Darkly tanned, Tennes has a straight nose and a square chin, with—you guessed it!—a Kirk Douglas cleft. Tennes oozes masculinity and virility. He's a handsome son-of-a-gun!

Personality traits:
A shrewd, ruthless business tycoon, Tennes is a man of strength and principle. He's perfected the art of buying floundering companies and turning them around financially, then selling them at a profit. He possesses a sixth sense about business—in short, he's a winner! But there are two sides to his personality. Always in cool command, Tennes, who fears no man or challenge, is rendered emotionally vulnerable when faced with his elderly aunt's illness. His deep devotion to the woman who raised him clearly casts him as a warm, compassionate guy—not at all like the tough-as-nails executive image he presents. Leave it to heroine Whitney Jordan to discover the real man behind the complicated enigma.

Heroine:
WHITNEY JORDAN's russet-colored hair floats past her shoulders in glorious waves. Her emerald green eyes, full breasts, and long, slender legs—not to mention her peaches-

and-cream complexion—make her eye-poppingly attractive. How can Tennes resist the twenty-six-year-old beauty? And how can Whitney consider becoming serious with him? If their romance flourishes, she may end up being Whitney Whitney!

Setting: Los Angeles, California

The Story:
One moment writer Whitney Jordan was strolling the aisles of McNeil's Department Store, plotting the untimely demise of a soap opera heartthrob; the next, she was nearly knocked over by a real-life stunner who implored her to be his fiancée! The ailing little gray-haired aunt who'd raised him had one final wish, he said—to see her dear nephew Tennes married to the wonderful girl he'd described in his letters . . . only that girl hadn't existed—until now! Tennes promised the masquerade would last only through lunch, but Whitney gave such an inspired performance that Aunt Olive refused to let her go. And what began as a playful romantic deception grew more breathlessly real by the minute. . . .

Cover Scene:
Whitney's living room is bright and cheerful. The gray carpeting and blue sofa with green and blue throw pillows gives the apartment a cool but welcoming appearance. Sitting on the sofa next to Tennes, Whitney is wearing a black crepe dress that is simply cut but stunning. It is cut low over her breasts and held at the shoulders by thin straps. The skirt falls to her knees in soft folds and the bodice is nipped in at the waist with a matching belt. She has on black high heels, but prefers not to wear any jewelry to spoil the simplicity of the dress. Tennes is dressed in a black suit with a white silk shirt and a deep red tie.

THE HOMETOWN HUNK CONTEST

FOR THE LOVE OF SAMI
(Originally Published as LOVESWEPT #34)
By Fayrene Preston

COVER NOTES

Hero:
DANIEL PARKER-ST. JAMES is every woman's dream come true. With glossy black hair and warm, reassuring blue eyes, he makes our heroine melt with just a glance. Daniel's lean face is chiseled into assertive planes. His lips are full and firmly sculptured, and his chin has the determined and arrogant thrust to it only a man who's sure of himself can carry off. Daniel has a lot in common with Clark Kent. Both wear glasses, and when Daniel removes them to make love to Sami, she thinks he really is Superman!

Personality traits:
Daniel Parker-St. James is one of the Twin Cities' most respected attorneys. He's always in the news, either in the society columns with his latest society lady, or on the front page with his headline cases. He's brilliant and takes on only the toughest cases—usually those that involve millions of dollars. Daniel has a reputation for being a deadly opponent in the courtroom. Because he's from a socially prominent family and is a Harvard graduate, it's expected that he'll run for the Senate one day. Distinguished-looking and always distinctively dressed—he's fastidious about his appearance—Daniel gives off an unassailable air of authority and absolute control.

Heroine:
SAMUELINA (SAMI) ADKINSON is secretly a wealthy heiress. No one would guess. She lives in a converted warehouse loft, dresses to suit no one but herself, and dabbles in the creative arts. Sami is twenty-six years old, with

long, honey-colored hair. She wears soft, wispy bangs and has very thick brown lashes framing her golden eyes. Of medium height, Sami has to look up to gaze into Daniel's deep blue eyes.

Setting: St. Paul, Minnesota

The Story:
Unpredictable heiress Sami Adkinson had endeared herself to the most surprising people—from the bag ladies in the park she protected . . . to the mobster who appointed himself her guardian . . . to her exasperated but loving friends. Then Sami was arrested while demonstrating to save baby seals, and it took powerful attorney Daniel Parker-St. James to bail her out. Daniel was smitten, soon cherishing Sami and protecting her from her night fears. Sami reveled in his love—and resisted it too. And holding on to Sami, Daniel discovered, was like trying to hug quicksilver. . . .

Cover Scene:
The interior of Daniel's house is very grand and supremely formal, the decor sophisticated, refined, and quietly tasteful, just like Daniel himself. Rich traditional fabrics cover plush oversized custom sofas and Regency wing chairs. Queen Anne furniture is mixed with Chippendale and is subtly complemented with Oriental accent pieces. In the library, floor-to-ceiling bookcases filled with rare books provide the backdrop for Sami and Daniel's embrace. Sami is wearing a gold satin sheath gown. The dress has a high neckline, but in back is cut provocatively to the waist. Her jewels are exquisite. The necklace is made up of clusters of flowers created by large, flawless diamonds. From every cluster a huge, perfectly matched teardrop emerald hangs. The earrings are composed of an even larger flower cluster, and an equally huge teardrop-shaped emerald hangs from each one. Daniel is wearing a classic, elegant tuxedo.

LOVESWEPT® HOMETOWN HUNK CONTEST

OFFICIAL RULES

> IN A CLASS BY ITSELF by Sandra Brown
> FOR THE LOVE OF SAMI by Fayrene Preston
> C.J.'S FATE by Kay Hooper
> THE LADY AND THE UNICORN by Iris Johansen
> CHARADE by Joan Elliott Pickart
> DARLING OBSTACLES by Barbara Boswell

1. NO PURCHASE NECESSARY. Enter the HOMETOWN HUNK contest by completing the Official Entry Form below and enclosing a sharp color full-length photograph (easy to see details, with the photo being no smaller than 2½" × 3½") of the man you think perfectly represents one of the heroes from the above-listed books which are described in the accompanying Loveswept cover notes. Please be sure to fill out the Official Entry Form completely, and also be sure to clearly print on the back of the man's photograph the man's name, address, city, state, zip code, telephone number, date of birth, your name, address, city, state, zip code, telephone number, your relationship, if any, to the man (e.g. wife, girlfriend) as well as the title of the Loveswept book for which you are entering the man. If you do not have an Official Entry Form, you can print all of the required information on a 3" × 5" card and attach it to the photograph with all the necessary information printed on the back of the photograph as well. YOUR HERO MUST SIGN BOTH THE BACK OF THE OFFICIAL ENTRY FORM (OR 3" × 5" CARD) AND THE PHOTOGRAPH TO SIGNIFY HIS CONSENT TO BEING ENTERED IN THE CONTEST. Completed entries should be sent to:

> BANTAM BOOKS
> HOMETOWN HUNK CONTEST
> Department CN
> 666 Fifth Avenue
> New York, New York 10102–0023

All photographs and entries become the property of Bantam Books and will not be returned under any circumstances.

2. Six men will be chosen by the Loveswept authors as a HOMETOWN HUNK (one HUNK per Loveswept title). By entering the contest, each winner and each person who enters a winner agrees to abide by Bantam Books' rules and to be subject to Bantam Books' eligibility requirements. Each winning HUNK and each person who enters a winner will be required to sign all papers deemed necessary by Bantam Books before receiving any prize. Each winning HUNK will be flown via **United Airlines** from his closest United Airlines-serviced city to New York City and will stay at the ▪▪▪▪ Sᴛᴀɴʜᴏᴘᴇ Hotel—the ideal hotel for business or pleasure in midtown Manhattan—for two nights. Winning HUNKS' meals and hotel transfers will be provided by Bantam Books. Travel and hotel arrangements are made by *RELIABLE TRAVEL INTERNATIONAL, INC* and are subject to availability and to Bantam Books' date requirements. Each winning HUNK will pose with a female model at a photographer's studio for a photograph that will serve as the basis of a Loveswept front cover. Each winning HUNK will receive a $150.00 modeling fee. Each winning HUNK will be required to sign an Affidavit of Eligibility and Model's Release supplied by Bantam Books. (Approximate retail value of HOMETOWN HUNK'S PRIZE: $900.00). The six people who send in a winning HOMETOWN HUNK photograph that is used by Bantam will receive free for one year each, LOVESWEPT romance paperback books published by Bantam during that year. (Approximate retail value: $180.00.) Each person who submits a winning photograph

will also be required to sign an Affidavit of Eligibility and Promotional Release supplied by Bantam Books. All winning HUNKS' (as well as the people who submit the winning photographs) names, addresses, biographical data and likenesses may be used by Bantam Books for publicity and promotional purposes without any additional compensation. There will be no prize substitutions or cash equivalents made.

3. All completed entries must be received by Bantam Books no later than September 15, 1988. Bantam Books is not responsible for lost or misdirected entries. The finalists will be selected by Loveswept editors and the six winning HOMETOWN HUNKS will be selected by the six authors of the participating Loveswept books. Winners will be selected on the basis of how closely the judges believe they reflect the descriptions of the books' heroes. Winners will be notified on or about October 31, 1988. If there are insufficient entries or if in the judges' opinions, no entry is suitable or adequately reflects the descriptions of the hero(s) in the book(s), Bantam may decide not to award a prize for the applicable book(s) and may reissue the book(s) at its discretion.

4. The contest is open to residents of the U.S. and Canada, except the Province of Quebec, and is void where prohibited by law. All federal and local regulations apply. Employees of Reliable Travel International, Inc., United Airlines, the Summit Hotel, and the Bantam Doubleday Dell Publishing Group, Inc., their subsidiaries and affiliates, and their immediate families are ineligible to enter.

5. For an extra copy of the Official Rules, the Official Entry Form, and the accompanying Loveswept cover notes, send your request and a self-addressed stamped envelope (Vermont and Washington State residents need not affix postage) before August 20, 1988 to the address listed in Paragraph 1 above.

LOVESWEPT® HOMETOWN HUNK OFFICIAL ENTRY FORM

BANTAM BOOKS
HOMETOWN HUNK CONTEST
Dept. CN
666 Fifth Avenue
New York, New York 10102–0023

HOMETOWN HUNK CONTEST

YOUR NAME_____

YOUR ADDRESS_____

CITY_____ STATE_____ ZIP_____

THE NAME OF THE LOVESWEPT BOOK FOR WHICH YOU ARE ENTERING THIS PHOTO

_____by_____

YOUR RELATIONSHIP TO YOUR HERO_____

YOUR HERO'S NAME_____

YOUR HERO'S ADDRESS_____

CITY_____ STATE_____ ZIP_____

YOUR HERO'S TELEPHONE #_____

YOUR HERO'S DATE OF BIRTH_____

YOUR HERO'S SIGNATURE CONSENTING TO HIS PHOTOGRAPH ENTRY

_____